MARDIE AND THE COCKINGTON GOLD

AN INSPECTOR FINDLAY MYSTERY

KEN MACKENZIE

OLD MATE MEDIA

CONTENTS

Chapter 1   1

Chapter 2   4

Chapter 3   18

Chapter 4   20

Chapter 5   23

Chapter 6   31

Chapter 7   36

Chapter 8   39

Chapter 9   42

Chapter 10   46

Chapter 11   51

Chapter 12   57

Chapter 13   65

Chapter 14   72

Chapter 15   77

Chapter 16   82

Chapter 17   89

Chapter 18   92

Chapter 19	96
Chapter 20	100
Chapter 21	107
Chapter 22	112
Chapter 23	115
Chapter 24	121
Chapter 25	125
Chapter 26	129
Chapter 27	136
Chapter 28	143
Chapter 29	145
Chapter 30	150
Chapter 31	154
Chapter 32	160
Chapter 33	162
Chapter 34	163
Chapter 35	167
Chapter 36	171
Chapter 37	179
Chapter 38	184
Chapter 39	193
Chapter 40	196
Postscript	208
Ken Mackenzie	221
Turn your book dreams into reality	222

CHAPTER I

Inspector Findlay sat quietly in his office, reading the Sunday paper. His old station clock ticking aloud like a beating drum. He was engrossed in a report of a burglary at Chelston Manor; a fifteenth century estate which lay midway between Torquay town and Cockington village.

Suddenly, there was a loud knock on his glass office door. Findlay jumped to his feet with a start. "Hello," he mumbled. "Who's there?" but there was no answer.

He walked over to the door and pulled it open. To his amazement, standing in front of him was Lady Victoria Preston. Once Lady of Chelston Manor until her husband, Lord David Preston, found more comfort with his secretary, Hannah.

"Lady Victoria," exclaimed Findlay. "Please come in."

She slowly walked past Findlay. The smell of her perfume seemed to fill his whole office. She looked like she belonged on the cover of one of Mrs Findlay's glossy magazines, he thought to himself. She was tall and slim with auburn hair tied back in a ponytail, which reached to her waist.

"Please," said Findlay, "have a seat."

She slowly sat down and began removing her white satin gloves.

"Inspector," she said quietly. "I need your help."

Findlay walked around his desk and settled into his large leather chair. He leaned forward and clasped his hands. "So," he said. "What can I do for you?"

Lady Victoria sat for a few seconds smoothing out her gloves, then said, "it's my husband, Lord David, he's disappeared."

Findlay raised his eyebrow. "Disappeared?" he repeated. "May I ask what makes you say disappeared?"

"Two days ago, he went for a walk around the estate; nobody has seen him since. I've had all our staff out looking for him. He has simply vanished."

For the first time, she raised her eyes and looked directly at Findlay.

Findlay sat for a few seconds, then cleared his throat. A habit he had when struggling to find the right words or was quietly embarrassed.

"I was just reading the report in the Express. Seems you were burgled?"

"Yes," she replied. "We were."

Findlay sat back in his chair. "May I ask why you didn't report it to the police?"

"We did," she replied. "David is a friend of the chief superintendent. He rang him."

Findlay shook his head. "I wasn't informed," he said.

"There was nothing to tell, Inspector, not really. They didn't take anything."

Findlay sat bolt upright. "Why would anybody break in and steal nothing? That doesn't make sense. When was this?"

"Three or maybe four days ago," she replied.

Findlay stood up and walked to the window. He stood for a few seconds, then turned around to face Lady Victoria. "When did you say you last saw Lord Preston?"

"Two days ago," she replied. "He often stays out all night, Inspector. I'm sure you've heard the rumours."

Findlay again cleared his throat. "Yes, quite."

"He always comes home, Inspector, always."

Just then, they heard the clatter of feet running up the wooden staircase to Findlay's office. The glass door swung open. It was Sergeant Allan Todd; Cockington's only other detective, as well as friend and colleague to Inspector Findlay.

CHAPTER 2

"Morning sir!" he shouted. "God awful out there, pis-sativly possing down!" he shouted.

He stopped dead and stared at the back of the woman sitting in front of Findlay. He closed his eyes and shook his head.

"Sorry sir. Excuse me, madam, I didn't see you there."

Findlay closed his eyes for a moment and shook his head. "Sergeant Todd, this is Lady Victoria Preston."

Todd stood motionless.

"Good morning," she said, holding out her hand.

"Pleased to meet you, your highness."

Lady Victoria raised an eyebrow and smiled.

"She's not the Queen, Sergeant, your ladyship will do."

"Sorry," said Todd, red faced.

"Now," said Findlay, "where were we? Oh yes, your husband. I have to be honest; you were quite right, I've heard the rumours."

"Maybe he just went to stay with friends."

Sergeant Todd sat for a second, looking confused. "Excuse me," said Todd, "are we talking about Lord Preston?"

"Yes," replied Findlay.

"Doesn't he drive a maroon-coloured Rolls Royce? I've seen him around the village on occasions."

"Yes, he does," replied Lady Victoria.

"Well," said Todd, "I just saw his car heading up towards Walnut Road and the Manor. I hate to say it sir, but by the way he was weaving, I think he may have been drinking."

Findlay's eyes opened wide. "There you are, your ladyship; seems the mystery is solved."

She stood up and collected her gloves from Findlay's desk. "Seems I was wasting your time, Inspector."

"Not at all," said Findlay. "Can I get my sergeant to take you back to the Manor?"

Todd's face lit up at the thought of spending some time with a beautiful woman.

"That would be very kind of you, thank you," she said.

Todd escorted her down the old wooden staircase to the street. "It's starting to rain again," said Todd. "Wait here, madame, I'll get the car."

Todd quickly made his way to the Drum Inn car park to collect Cockington's one and only police car.

He jumped in and drove the short distance to Inspector Findlay's office. He climbed out, umbrella in hand, and held it over Lady Victoria's head. Todd pulled open the passenger door while she climbed in.

He couldn't help himself. He glanced down at her long legs; he just couldn't resist. "Damn," he muttered, closing the door. "She saw me. Damn it. Damn, damn, damn!"

Todd climbed into the driver's seat. He sat for a couple of seconds, which felt like a lifetime.

He was about to apologise for his indiscretion, when she suddenly said, "Come along, Sergeant, let's go."

Todd took a deep breath. *Maybe she didn't see me*, he thought.

Todd turned the engine over. "On or off?" he said.

"I beg your pardon, Sergeant?"

"The police siren. Would you like it on or off?"

"I'm not twelve!" said Lady Victoria. She took a deep breath. "Just drive Sergeant. Just drive."

They began their journey back to Chelston Manor, the home of Lord Preston.

"So, Sergeant, you work on a Sunday?"

"Yes. Erm, I mean no."

"Well," she said, "which is it?"

"I wasn't working," replied Todd. "I knew the inspector would be on his own. Sunday is Mrs Findlay's flower day. She goes up to Jack Mullen's place for flower arranging club. I just called into the office to say hello."

"Doesn't your wife mind you leaving her alone on a Sunday?"

"Oh, I'm not married," said Todd.

"Really?" she replied. "A girlfriend perhaps?"

"No," said Todd. "No girlfriend."

Lady Victoria smiled. "Well, Sergeant," she said. "A good-looking man like you. How unusual."

Todd could feel his face starting to burn.

Lady Victoria smiled. "Touché Sergeant?"

Todd looked at her blankly.

"I take it you don't speak French, Sergeant?"

"Erm, no, I'm afraid not," he said. "To be honest, I sometimes struggle with English."

She smiled. "Do you live in the village?" she asked.

"Yes, I do. I've been here seven years."

She didn't reply, she just nodded.

"What about you?" said Todd. "Is it true you live in the annex at Preston Manor?"

Lady Victoria just stared out of the window.

Then she said, "So, I'm the talk of Cockington, am I?"

"No, I don't think so," said Todd.

Nothing was said for a few seconds.

"I'm sorry," he said. "I didn't mean to pry. Is it front or back?"

"Front or back what?" she snapped.

"Do I drop you at the front, or the Annex at the back?"

"My husband may be a cheating pig, Sergeant, but I'm still Lady Victoria Preston. Front door will be perfect!"

Todd slowly pulled up in front of Chelston Manor, which, at one time, sat in over five hundred acres of woodland. Lord Preston's family had lived there since the mid-seventeenth century.

Unfortunately, with funds running low, not much in the way of maintenance had been done in years. The manor was looking a lot worse for the Devonshire weather.

Todd pulled up at the large oak doorway and jumped out. He opened the passenger door and offered his hand.

Lady Victoria took it and climbed out. Todd made a point of averting his eyes and not looking down.

She smiled, and said, "Well done, Sergeant."

Todd could feel his face burning up. *So, she did see me*, he thought to himself. *Damn.*

"Thank you for the lift, Sergeant," she said.

Todd looked up at the front of the manor. It looked shabby and in need of some serious renovation. "Shouldn't there be a staff member to assist you?" asked Todd.

"No," she replied. "Every penny counts these days."

Todd nodded. "Of course. I'll be on my way then."

"Wait," she said. "Would you mind seeing me in?"

"Yes, of course I will," said Todd. He offered her his arm, and they both climbed the marble steps towards the arched doors.

"Unfortunately not, Sergeant, it's this way." She said, pointing to the Annex.

"Oh right," said Todd. "So, you do live in the annex?"

"I'm afraid so. To be truthful, Sergeant, it's better than sharing the house with that family."

They walked across the gravel driveway of the main court-yard towards the garages and stables.

"That's strange," she said. "The end garage should be open. It's always open, and there's a light on."

Todd walked over and yanked on the garage door. It swung up, allowing billowing smoke and fumes to pour out. Inside was Lord Preston's Rolls Royce, doors and windows firmly shut.

"Oh, my god!" said Lady Victoria. "Is he in there? Please tell me he isn't."

"There's somebody inside," said Todd. "I can't make out who." He pulled open the car door and smoke poured out. He reached in and pulled a lifeless body out.

Lady Victoria screamed. It was Hannah Winton, Lord Preston's secretary.

Todd fell to his knees, checking for any sign of life. There was none.

"Do you have a phone in the Annex?" asked Todd.

"Yes, I do."

The pair quickly made their way into the annex kitchen, where Todd rang for an ambulance. He then rang Inspector Findlay.

"I'm on my way," said Findlay. "Have you rung for an ambulance?"

"Yes, sir."

"Well done," he said. "I'll be there as quickly as I can."

Todd had just put the phone down when, from the corner of his eye, he saw somebody in the garden. "Hey there!" he shouted.

There was no answer. He ran into the undergrowth and again he shouted, "This is the police! Who's there?"

There was still no answer. Just the crackling and rustling of the undergrowth.

Lady Victoria joined him. "Who was it?"

"I have no idea," said Todd. He gestured towards the annex. "We may as well go back inside, we can wait for the inspector to get here."

They both made their way back to the kitchen.

"My god," said Lady Victoria. "Why would she do such a thing? She wasn't one of my favourite people, Sergeant, but I wouldn't have wished that on her. I don't understand."

Just then, they heard a car pulling up. It was Findlay.

"Well, Sergeant, seems I can't leave you alone without you finding trouble. Show me," said Findlay.

"This way, sir."

The two men made their way across the courtyard to the garages. Todd explained what had happened and how they found her.

They reached the garage; the smell of exhaust fumes still filled the air. Findlay knelt down and checked for a pulse, but there wasn't one.

"Do we know where Lord Preston is?" asked Findlay.

"I don't know, sir, we haven't seen him."

"There's obviously nothing we can do here." He stood up, shrugged his shoulders and gestured to Todd to leave.

They walked slowly back to the annex, where Lady Victoria was standing on the steps.

"Lady Victoria," said Findlay. "Where can I find Lord Preston?"

"I have no idea, Inspector, possibly in the main house."

"When you saw Lord Preston's car, Sergeant, was he driving it?"

"I wouldn't know, sir; I only saw the back of it."

Findlay turned to Lady Victoria. "Who else lives in the manor?" he asked.

"Lord David, of course, and his two sons, Robert and Edward, not forgetting Hannah."

"Not anymore," said Todd.

Findlay glared at him.

"Sorry sir," said Todd.

Inspector Findlay said nothing.

He turned back to Lady Victoria. "What about staff?" asked Findlay.

"There's Madge the cook, Simonds, Lord Preston's valet, oh and Mardie, she's the gardener. She sometimes has help from the men in the village. She's lived and worked at Chelston Manor since she was little. Her mother and father were the cook and gardener here for years, but that's everyone, Inspector. Thanks to government taxes and the cost of labour these days, we were lucky the manor wasn't turned into a hotel or an asylum years ago."

"Right," said Findlay. "Come along, Sergeant."

They turned and made their way across the gravelled courtyard towards Chelston Manor.

"Look at this place," said Findlay. "Look at the size of it! The electricity bill alone must be more than I earn in a year."

Todd just nodded.

"There is one thing I should mention, sir," said Todd. "Just before you arrived, there was someone in the woods. I did go after whoever it was, but I lost them."

"We will deal with one problem at a time, Sergeant. I am still trying to work out why somebody would break in and not steal anything, doesn't make any sense, and now this."

Just then, they heard the ringing of a bell. "It's the ambulance, Sergeant. You better go and meet it. I'll find his Lordship."

Todd turned on his heel and hurried towards the main gates to await the emergency services.

Inspector Findlay climbed the steps toward the white marble pillars of Chelston Manor. He couldn't help thinking back to when he first arrived in Cockington. One of his first call outs was here. Suspected burglary. Findlay smiled. It turned out to be a couple of the village kids stealing sticks of rhubarb from the kitchen garden. "Over thirty years ago," he said to himself.

Findlay was now standing in front of the huge arch shaped oak doors. *No point in knocking,* he thought to himself. He pushed on one side of the doors and they slowly opened.

Findlay walked in.

The first thing that struck him was the smell; musty, damp.

He walked into the entrance hall. For a few seconds, he stood wide eyed looking up at the domed ceiling. *Good god,* he thought, *it's like entering the Sistine Chapel.*

He looked half way up the circular marble staircase and there was the biggest painting he had ever seen. It covered the entire wall and stairwell. He was mesmerised looking at all the characters in it, a battle scene.

"Looks like Waterloo," he muttered.

Suddenly, the silence was broken.

"Stop right there!" said a voice.

It was Simonds, the valet come butler. "What the hell do you think you're doing in here?" he said. "You can't just walk in!"

"The door was open," replied Findlay.

"Like hell it was," said Simonds. "I'll ask again, what do you want?"

Findlay pulled out his warrant card. "My name is..."

Simonds interrupted him, "I know who you are, for god's sake! Now, what do you want?"

Findlay glared at him for a few seconds. "I wish to speak with Lord Preston."

"Then make an appointment," said Simonds. "It's late."

Findlay looked down at his trusty old watch. "It's only just after eleven in the morning. Besides, it's never too late for the police," growled Findlay. "Suppose I just take you and his lordship down to the police station?"

Just then, another voice echoed around the great entrance hall. It was Lord David Preston.

"That's enough Simonds," he shouted. "I'll see the Inspector in my study."

Simonds glared at Findlay.

"Very well, sir," he said with a growl. "Please come this way, Inspector."

He turned and walked towards yet more large arched oak doors.

Findlay followed him. They entered the main study, an imposing room stuck in a time warp.

Findlay couldn't help but think it was like stepping back into an early Victorian library. Dark oak panelling on one side with family paintings adorning every space. On the other side of the room were more books than Torquay Library, Findlay thought to himself. At the far end of the room, Lord Preston stood in front of a roaring fire that crackled and spat out amber sparks. He was standing with one hand resting on the overhanging fireplace shelf, drumming his fingers.

"So, Inspector, what can I do for you?"

"Good afternoon, sir. I am the bearer of bad news, I'm afraid. Perhaps we could sit?"

"By all means, Inspector. May I get you a drink? Scotch? Or even a Tea?"

"No thank you," said Findlay. "I'm here about Miss Winton."

"Hannah?" exclaimed Lord Preston. "What about her?"

"Yes sir, Hannah Winton."

"Could I ask when you last saw her?"

"Not since last night," replied Preston. "We had a row. It was nothing really, but she stormed off. Be about eight pm. Why do you ask? Is she in trouble?"

"I'm afraid the body of Miss Winton has just been discovered in one of your garages."

Lord Preston stood motionless for a few seconds. He said nothing.

Findlay simply sat and stared at him.

Preston walked over to his drinks cabinet and poured himself a large whiskey.

He still said nothing. He took a drink from the glass, then said, "How?"

"I'm not sure yet," said Findlay. "Emergency services are on their way from Torquay. My sergeant is with her now. At this point, it looks like she may have taken her own life."

"I don't understand," said Preston. "We had a simple argument, something and nothing."

"May I ask when you last used your car?"

"A couple of days ago. Why?"

Findlay didn't answer.

"Does anyone else have access to the car keys?"

"Just Simonds, and my wife, I suppose, or at least she knows where I keep them."

Just then, Findlay heard a floorboard creak. He reached out and yanked open the study door. It was Simonds, Lord Preston's Valet.

"Anything I can do for you?" said Findlay sarcastically.

"No", said Simonds sheepishly. "Not really."

Findlay pushed the door closed while Simonds stood looking in. It clicked shut.

"Take no notice of Simonds, Inspector. He's very protective. He is harmless. He's been with the family since I was a little boy."

"So, what happens now?" said Preston.

"The area will be off limits for the time being, at least for the rest of the day. I will need to speak with you again," said Findlay. "And anyone else who lives in the house."

"Yes Inspector, of course."

Findlay picked up his trilby hat and gave it a brush with the back of his hand. "I'll bid you good day for now, sir." And he left.

He was only halfway to the front door when a hushed voice said. "Here. Over here."

Findlay was startled for a second. "Who's there?" he demanded.

"Shush," said the voice. "Over here."

He could barely make out a figure in the darkness of the hallway. It was standing with a door half opened beckoning. "Over here," it said again.

Findlay made his way over. "Who is it?" he demanded again.

"In here," said the voice. "Quickly."

Findlay walked through a doorway into what looked like the back of the old Victorian kitchen; with copper pans and cooking utensils hanging from every one of the timber ceiling beams. It reminded him of a medieval torture chamber. He could now see a dishevelled outline of a woman. She was wearing a pair of old green wellington boots, and an old army style long grey coat held together with a cloth belt.

"Who are you?" demanded Findlay.

"My name's Mardie," she said. "I be the gardener here. I looks after the gardens and stuff for his lordship."

"Is she dead?" she asked.

"Is who dead?" replied Findlay.

"Her. That woman. She hasn't been here for two shakes of a lamb's tail and got her claws into his lordship. So, is she dead?"

"I'm afraid she is," replied Findlay. "I take it you didn't like her very much, Mardie, is it?"

"Yes, it be Mardie, and no, I damn well didn't," she said.

Findlay couldn't help but notice she wasn't the best kept woman he had ever seen. Her hair was straggled and greasy, and she had more earth under her fingernails than on her boots. Findlay also recognised the smell of rotting manure; a smell he got every time he opened the doors to his greenhouse.

"So, Mardie, can you tell me anything that might help?"

For a moment, she said nothing. Then she said, "I was born here, you know."

"Yes, I know," he replied. "But can you tell me anything that might help me find out what happened here?"

Mardie said nothing. Then she said, "They be after the Chelston treasure, you know."

Findlay looked at her in astonishment. "What treasure is that, Mardie?"

"It's hidden here," she said. "In the manor."

Findlay was unsure what she was talking about. He decided it was best to just leave. Poor woman wasn't bound too tightly, he thought to himself.

Then it occurred to him. *How did she get into the manor?* He couldn't see Simonds allowing her indoors.

"I need to ask you a question," he said. "And I want you to be honest with me. It's very, very, important. Do you understand?"

"I do," she replied.

"A few nights ago, somebody entered the manor, but they didn't take anything. Whoever it was didn't use keys. The doors were bolted on the inside, as well as the windows. So, whoever it was, knows how to get in and out without being seen. Would that have been you, Mardie? Be sure to tell me the truth now."

For a few seconds, she stood nervously, scratching the back of her hand.

"I dint steal nothin. I dint break nothin."

"I know, Mardie, I know you didn't. Why would you come in at night when the household is sleeping? Why?"

"I gets cold and I gets hungry. Can't survive on potatoes and fruits from the garden, so I comes in now and then and gets me something to eat. Been doing it for years. They never caught me, not yet."

Findlay was stunned by her reply. On one hand, it solved a mystery, on the other hand it opened another.

"Thank you, Mardie," said Findlay. "I may need to speak with you again."

Mardie said nothing. She just stared at him.

Findlay turned and was about to leave when suddenly she said, "He did it."

Findlay stopped dead in his tracks. He walked back towards her.

"Who did what? Who are you talking about?"

"Him," she said again. "He did it. I saw him."

At that, she turned and disappeared into the shadows of a stairwell.

Findlay ran to the top of the stairs, but she had gone.

"Damn," he said out loud as he squinted to see down the dark passageway, but she had vanished.

Findlay stood for a few seconds, listening. He could hear the sound of hurried footsteps slowly becoming more distant. "Sounds like a passageway or a tunnel," he said to himself. He was tempted to follow, but decided against it. "A job for Sergeant Todd," he muttered.

He pulled the stairwell door closed and turned to leave.

"Sir," shouted a voice in the gloom of the hallway. It was Todd.

"For God's sake Todd," shouted Findlay. "You nearly gave me a heart attack."

"Sorry sir," said Todd.

"Well?" said Findlay. "What is it?"

"The ambulance is here, sir; they're taking Miss Winton away."

"Very well, Sergeant, lead on."

The two men made their way over to the garages. They arrived just as she was being put into the back of the coroner's van.

"The coroner's over there, sir."

"Right, Sergeant, thank you."

"Oh," said Findlay. "See if you can track down the gardener, Mardie, she's called. Have a chat with her about what she meant by; he did it."

"Did what sir?"

"I have no idea, Sergeant. Just something she said. I don't think she is wrapped too tightly, so be gentle with her."

"Yes sir," said Todd. "Where will I find her?"

"If I knew that, Sergeant, I wouldn't be asking you to go and look for her, would I?"

"No sir. You would not."

"Try the garden. After all, she is the Chelston Manor gardener."

"Yes sir," said Todd, as he headed off into the woods.

CHAPTER 3

Findlay walked towards the garages. "My god if it isn't Beth Middleton," he said with a surprised voice. "Haven't seen you in a year or two."

"If it isn't Sergeant Findlay."

"That's Inspector Findlay now Beth."

"Inspector? Well, well," she said sarcastically. "You have gone up in the world. It must be over thirty years; I'm amazed you recognised me!"

"How could I not?" said Findlay smiling. "So, Beth, you're the new Coroner?"

"Yes," she said in a sullen voice. "Even us women can climb the ladder of success."

Findlay laughed.

"It's been a long time Beth..."

"Since you left me standing in Paddington station waiting for you to show up, you mean?"

"Yes," said Findlay under his breath. "I do owe you an explanation."

"No," she interrupted. "You don't. At least nothing I care to hear. Let's just keep this professional, shall we, Inspector?"

"As you wish, Beth, as you wish."

"So, what can you tell me here?" asked Findlay.

She looked down at her notes. "I'll know more when I get a proper look at her. For now, I can tell you, death wasn't caused by asphyxiation. She was dead at least a couple of hours before being placed in the garage."

Findlay looked at her with a confused look on his face. "How can that be possible?" he said. "My sergeant saw Lord Preston driving up the hill in his Rolls just an hour before he found the body."

"I can't help you, Inspector. I can only give you the facts. Her skin colouring tells all. At this stage it's just a guess, but I would say, poisoned."

Findlay stood in silence while turning the winder on his watch, a habit he had for many years when things didn't make sense.

"Right," she said. "I'm all done here. I'll be in touch when I've done the post mortem. You'll have my report."

"Wait," said Findlay. "Meet me in the village later, and please allow me to explain Paddington."

She took a deep breath and slowly exhaled. "Very well, I'll meet you in the Drum Inn at seven."

She closed her briefcase with a loud click and brushed past him.

Findlay stood and watched as she climbed into her car and left.

CHAPTER 4

Todd made his way back to his car. The emergency services had left, so he decided to go back to the office in Cockington village. Inspector Findlay should be there by now, he thought. He drove out of the large iron gates and headed down the hill towards the village. It wasn't long before he reached the office of the Cockington constabulary.

He parked outside, climbed out, and slammed the car door.

"That won't do it any good," said a voice behind him. Todd looked over his shoulder. It was Sally, the barmaid from the Drum Inn in the village.

"Sal," he said with a smile. "You made me jump!"

"It's nice to know I can get some kind of reaction out of you," she said with a smile.

Todd knew he was blushing.

"Why Allan Todd, you're turning bright red."

He said nothing and just turned away.

"When are you going to stop fighting it, Allan? You know we are meant to be together," she said with a smile.

Todd's face grew ever more crimson.

Sally laughed as she passed him. "One day, Sergeant Todd," she shouted, "one day I'll get you down the aisle." And she headed for the Drum.

He watched her as she walked down towards the local pub.

Todd did as he always did and ran up the wooden staircase to Findlay's office two steps at a time. He pushed open the glass door and entered the office like a whirlwind.

"Got lots to tell you, sir."

Findlay slowly raised his head from the file he was reading and looked at Todd over his black-rimmed glasses.

"Tell me, Sergeant, does Mrs Bruce your landlady allow you to run up and down the stairs like that?"

"Actually sir, no, she doesn't."

"Then please refrain from doing it here."

"Yes sir, sorry sir."

"And Sergeant, stop saying sorry."

"Yes sir, sorry."

Findlay glared at him and shook his head. He put down his file and sat back in his seat.

"Right, he said, "what do you have to tell me?"

"Firstly, I think I might have solved the burglary at Chelston Manor."

"Really?" said Findlay. "Are you going to tell me it was Mardie, the gardener?"

Todd stood and stared. "Yes sir. How did you know?"

"She told me."

"Oh," said Todd.

"She goes in to steal food now and then. Seems the estate dog gets better treatment than she does."

"You have to see where she lives sir, it's literally a shed in the woods, and she pays rent for it to Robert Preston. I bet he wouldn't keep the estate dog in it. Have we had the post mortem report on Hannah Winton yet, sir?"

"Not yet," said Findlay. "I'm meeting the coroner this evening; I'm hoping she will have news for me."

"I hope you don't mind my asking, sir, but I got the impression you and the coroner knew each other?"

"You're correct Sergeant, we do know each other, but in a different life."

"Oh, I see," said Todd. "I take it this was long before you met Mrs Findlay?"

"Of course," said Findlay abruptly. "Long before."

"Sorry," said Todd.

"No need to apologise, Sergeant. It was a long time ago. So, Sergeant, back to the business in hand. What's your impression of Simonds, the valet?"

"I don't like him much, just something about him."

"Well," said Findlay. "He's been with the Preston family for decades."

"Is there a Mrs Simonds?" asked Todd.

"There is sergeant, or at least there was. They have been divorced for years, seems she caught him with one of the kitchen maids. All hell let loose and she moved out. I'm thinking maybe a call wouldn't go amiss, never know what you might find out, a woman scorned and all that."

"I have a meeting with the coroner at seven. It's after six already, let's call it a night," said Findlay. "Tomorrow is another day."

At that, Todd grabbed his coat, scarf, and hat and headed for the door.

"Sergeant."

"Yes sir?"

"Bright and early tomorrow. We have a busy day."

"I will be sir. Good night."

"Good Night," said Findlay as he sat forward in his chair and went back to reading his file.

CHAPTER 5

He was halfway through it when the old station clock that hung above his office door began to chime. Findlay realised he had fallen asleep; it was seven o'clock. He jumped up from his chair, grabbed his coat, and made his way out. He ran as quickly as he could down the stairs and into the street.

He looked at his watch, three minutes past seven. He could see the lights of the pub at the bottom of Cockington Lane. They seemed miles away. He knew Beth would be sitting waiting for him. He couldn't believe he was going to be late after all these years.

He ran as best he could down the hill towards the Drum Inn. The harder he ran, the further away the pub seemed to get. "Damn," he said. "Please still be there."

He reached the pub steps and began climbing them. He looked at his watch, six minutes past seven. "Not bad for an old man," he said, congratulating himself on his run.

He grabbed the pub door and pulled. It was like opening up another world. He was suddenly bathed in light from the pub lounge. The light spilled out onto the road as cigarette smoke gushed out from the open door.

Findlay stepped inside. As a tee-totaller, he rarely went into pubs. He stood for a moment, looking around the packed bar. As he walked through to the lounge, he waved his hand in front of his face to try to waft away the cigarette smoke that hung in the air.

He reached the public lounge and looked around. There in a corner booth was Beth.

Findlay walked slowly over. "Beth," he said with a smile.

She looked at her watch. "You're late. You were always late back then, too."

"I know," said Findlay. "Sorry. May I sit down?"

"If you would like to," she replied.

Findlay sat down and slid his way along the leather seat until he was sitting opposite her. For a few seconds, they sat and stared at each other.

It was Beth who broke the silence. "I'm waiting."

Findlay looked at her. "Waiting for what?" he said.

"Where's my apology?" she said.

"Ah, that," replied Findlay.

"Yes, that," she said.

"How long has it been?" asked Findlay. "Must be twenty-four, twenty-five years?"

"Try twenty-nine years and four months," she said.

"Oh," said Findlay.

"I'm still waiting," she said with a sarcastic smile.

"I'm sorry," said Findlay. "Please let me explain."

"You can try," she said.

"The day I left you standing in the station, it was an awful thing to do, and I do sincerely apologise. I had a call from an old flame. I was rather surprised, to be honest. She said she was in Plymouth for the day on business and wanted to meet up. I hadn't seen her for over two years."

"Do I really need to hear this?" interrupted Beth.

"Yes, I think you do," said Findlay.

"Her name is Mary."

"You just said...is...Mary," said Beth.

"Yes, a year or so later, we were married."

"Well," said Beth. "I wasn't expecting that."

Findlay continued with his story. "We spent the day just talking. I knew then I couldn't let her go, not again: I loved her, I always had. Then I realised the time. I knew you were waiting, but it was too late. I let you down, and I'm sorry. "

Beth sat for a second, then shook her head. "So," she said. "You owe me."

Findlay smiled. "Yes, I suppose I do."

"Doesn't mean I forgive you," she added. "In a way, you did me a favour. Had you not let me down, I wouldn't have met Alex."

"Alex?" said Findlay.

"Yes, on that day when you didn't arrive, I went for a tea. I was furious. I even had a little cry. Alex was sitting behind me. He asked if I was alright. We got chatting, and the rest is history. We have just celebrated our twenty-fifth anniversary."

"So," said Findlay. "There's always a silver lining."

"I suppose so," said Beth.

"Now down to business," she said. "My first assumptions were correct. She was poisoned."

"This is very confusing," said Findlay. "You're saying she was killed hours before, then placed in Preston's Rolls Royce, and made to look like a suicide."

"That's what it looks like to me," she said. "But then I'm not the detective."

Findlay sat back in his seat and stared at her for a second. Then he said, "So, when my sergeant saw Preston's car heading for the Manor, her body must have been in it. So, the question is, who on earth was driving?"

Beth closed her briefcase with a click. "Seems you have a murder on your hands."

"I'm sure with today's advances in medical science, it will only take a day or two to work out which poison it was. After all, we are not in the dark ages anymore. It is 1939, another decade starts in a few months. We've come a long way since you and I started out."

Beth stood up. "It's time I went," she said. "I'm sure we will see each other again now I'm based in Torquay. I'll have the report sent over as soon as I have it."

Findlay slowly arose from his seat. He reached out and took her hand. "Once again, I am sorry."

Beth smiled. She finished buttoning up her coat, gave him one last smile, and left.

Findlay watched as the heavy oak doors of the Drum Inn slammed behind her. He sat down and stared at the empty seat opposite him. He couldn't help remembering the good times he and Beth had had. They were both young, both at university, and both enjoying everything life threw at them.

Then his thoughts turned to Mrs Findlay, the love of his life. Reality brought him back into the real world. He smiled. "Think I will get home early tonight," he said to himself.

He was about to stand up and leave when Sally, the barmaid, appeared in front of him. Findlay was startled. "Steady on Sally," he said. "Give a man a coronary creeping up on him like that. What can I do for you?"

"It's Allan, your sergeant. I was wondering, Inspector, could you have a word with him?"

"A word," repeated Findlay. "What kind of a word? I hope he hasn't said or done anything to upset you? He can be a little thoughtless sometimes."

"No," said Sally. "Nothing like that. I've been after him ever since he arrived in Cockington, but he won't even ask me out for a drink. Can you speak to him, please?"

Findlay sat motionless and stared at her. "You want me to tell him to ask you out on a date?"

"Exactly!" said Sally enthusiastically.

Findlay took a deep breath. "Well Sally," he said. "It's not the kind of thing I would feel comfortable doing."

"Please Inspector, just tell him to ask me out for a drink. He will listen to you," she said, "Oh thank you inspector, thank you."

Before he could take a breath, she was gone. He stood for a few seconds wondering what on earth had just happened. He was trying to remember if he had agreed or not. He shook his head in bewilderment and made his way to the door.

"Goodnight, Inspector," shouted Sally. "And thank you."

Findlay smiled and looked blankly at her. He raised his hand and gave her a little wave. "Yes," he said. "Goodnight." And he left.

He climbed into his old Volvo, the second love of his life, and made his way home. He couldn't get Sally out of his mind. *Good God*, he thought to himself. *Did I actually agree to that?*

He arrived back at his home, Church Way cottage in the centre of Cockington Village. It always gave him a warm feeling when at the end of each day he went home to his loving wife, a roaring fire and a home cooked meal.

He put his key in the door and pushed. As soon as he stepped in, he could feel the warmth from the open fire which Mrs Findlay always made sure was burning when he got home.

The smell of smouldering wood and Mrs Findlay's beef stew wafted around the thatched cottage and always brought a smile to his face.

His wife came out of the Kitchen, "Hello darling," she said. "I didn't hear you come in.

Take your shoes off, dear. I've just cleaned the floor tiles. Your slippers are in front of the fire."

"Lovely," replied Findlay. "You do look after me, dear."

"I know," she said.

He slipped his shoes off and placed them neatly next to the front door and pulled on his favourite comfy slippers. He went into the kitchen and sat down at the table. Mrs Findlay was standing at the cooker stirring the stew.

"Won't be long dear," she said.

"Thank you," replied Findlay. "It smells wonderful."

"You're very quiet tonight," she said. "Have you had a hard day?"

"It's been an interesting day, yes. I had a meeting with the coroner earlier this evening," he said. "It was Beth."

"Beth who?" she asked.

"Beth Middleton," said Findlay.

"Well gracious me, that's a name from the past," said Mrs Findlay.

"Yes," he said. "I was quite taken aback when I saw her."

"Really. Did it bring back memories for you?" she said with a grin.

Findlay smiled. "Not really dear, you know I only have eyes for you. Besides, it's been nearly thirty years."

Mrs Findlay didn't reply. She shrugged off the thought of his old girlfriend and changed the subject.

"So, what has been happening around Torquay on this bright and sunny Sunday she asked?"

"Not good," replied Findlay. "The body of a young girl, Hannah Winton, was found today up at Chelston Manor."

"Good heavens," she said, "poor girl."

"Yes," said Findlay. "It was my sergeant, Allan, who found her."

"Poor Allan," she replied. "Is he alright? It's not right that young people should see things like that."

Findlay smiled. "All part of the job, dear."

"Yes," she replied. "I know."

"While we are on the subject of Allan Todd," said Findlay. "I had a very strange conversation with Sally from the Drum." He went on to tell her what Sally had asked him to do.

Mrs Findlay burst out laughing. "She certainly picked the wrong one to carry that message."

"Well, don't just sit there laughing," said Findlay. "What should I do?"

She finally composed herself. "It's just the thought of you discussing affairs of the heart with Allan. I would love to be a fly on the wall when that conversation takes place. I'm sorry for laughing, dear," she said with a grin. "But it is amusing."

"So, what should I do?"

"Just simply tell him what you just told me. Then ask him for a date." She started laughing again.

"Oh, do behave!" said Findlay. "You're really not helping."

"I have an idea," she said. "Invite Allan round for a meal. I will see Sally in the village, and I will invite her. We will get them both together in a neutral meeting place, here, then we will leave them to it. I'll prepare a nice cooked meal for them."

"Do we have to be here?" asked Findlay.

"No, we don't, because you will take me to the Grand Hotel in town, and buy me dinner for getting you out of a hole."

"And that," said Findlay, "is why I love you. You can fix anything!"

"Right," she said. "Tomorrow night at seven. Be sure he comes and is on time. I don't want Sally sitting here on her own."

"I will make sure he is on time, you can depend on it," he said.

CHAPTER 6

The next morning, Findlay arrived at his office at 8. 00am. He was never late and believed in leading by example.

Almost as soon as he arrived, his office phone began ringing. "That's early," he muttered. He quickly unbuttoned his top coat, took off his scarf, and hung them on the coat stand. He picked up the phone. "Good morning," he said. "Findlay here. How can I help?"

A voice on the other end said, "That sounds very official for eight in the morning." It was the coroner, Beth Middleton.

"Beth," he said. "What a surprise. What can I do for you?"

"It's more a case of what I can do for you," she said. "I've had your autopsy report back. It's a strange one. Buy me lunch at the Drum, I'll run through it with you."

"Lunch it is," said Findlay. "How does twelve suit?"

"It does," she replied. "See you then." And she hung up.

Findlay suddenly felt a cloak of guilt wrap itself around him. "It will be fine," he mumbled. "It's just lunch, it's business." But it didn't stop him feeling guilty.

Just then the office door sprung open. It was Todd.

"Morning, sir," he said with his usual enthusiasm.

"Good morning to you, Sergeant."

"Are we any the wiser, sir?"

"Not really," replied Findlay. "The autopsy report is in, so maybe that will shed some light on how that poor girl met her end."

"Before I forget," he said, "Mrs Findlay has invited you to dinner at our house, tonight at seven."

"Oh right," said Todd. "Thank you, that's very kind of her, you as well, sir."

Findlay grunted. "Seven o'clock," he said with a smile.

"I'll let Mrs Bruce know I won't be home for dinner."

"And Sergeant," said Findlay, "do not be late!"

"Understand, yes sir, of course."

"Good," said Findlay, "because my life wouldn't be worth living if you turn up late."

Todd looked at him inquisitively. "Sorry sir."

"It's nothing Sergeant, just don't be late."

"Who in the village knows everything about everyone?" said Findlay. "There's always one in every village who knows it all. That's your job this morning, Sergeant; go and find me the local gossip. I want to know all there is to know about Chelston Manor and its landed gentry. Something doesn't feel right. I can't quite put my finger on it, but I'm getting an uneasy feeling about the Preston family."

"I think I know someone who will know who I have to speak to, my landlady Mrs Bruce. If she doesn't know, nobody will."

"Then I will leave it in your capable hands, Sergeant, and remember, seven sharp. Do not be late."

Todd made his way home to speak with Mrs Bruce. She had been his landlady for seven years, ever since he was posted to Cockington Village. He opened the front door and shouted, "Hello? Mrs Bruce, are you home?"

She suddenly appeared at the top of the stairs. "For heaven's sake, Allan," she said, "you frightened the life out of me shouting like that. Whatever is the matter?"

Mrs Bruce had lived in Cockington for over fifty years, ever since she and her husband moved down from Glasgow. She had run the village's only B&B since her husband died over twenty years ago and looked on Allan Todd as more of a grandson than a paying guest.

"I need to pick your brains," he said to her. "Gossip."

She looked at him with a stunned look. "I beg your pardon," she muttered.

"No," said Todd. "I didn't mean you."

"I'm glad to hear it," she replied.

"What on earth are you talking about, laddie?" she asked in her rustic Glaswegian accent, which always put Todd on his guard. It usually meant he was in trouble.

"I need to ask you something," he said.

"Ask away," she said. "But make it quick, I'm in the middle of bleaching your toilet."

"Oh," said Todd. "Thanks."

"Well? I haven't got all day. What is it you want?"

"Who in the village knows everything about everyone and everything?"

"Well," she said, "now you're asking something. Who is it you're trying to find out about?"

"I can't say," said Todd. "It's an ongoing investigation."

"That will be the Prestons then, and that poor lassie they found in his Lordship's car."

Todd was speechless. "But how?"

"Don't ask," she said. "I haven't lived here for half a century without knowing a few people who know a few people," she smiled. "I'll put the kettle on, shall I?"

Todd sat at the kitchen table. "While I think of it," he said, "I've been invited to Inspector Findlay's house tonight for a meal."

Mrs Bruce stopped rinsing the tea cups and turned around. "Why?" she asked.

Todd laughed. "What do you mean, why?! Maybe because they like me."

Mrs Bruce squinted her eyes. "Was it him or his wife who invited you?" she said.

"Well, actually, I think it was Mrs Findlay."

"Then there's more to it than dinner," she said.

"I'm worried now," said Todd.

Mrs Bruce placed the tray with a teapot and milk jug on the table and sat down.

"Now then, laddie, what is it you want to know?"

Todd finished pouring his tea. "This must stay between us," he insisted.

"Of course," said Mrs Bruce, "I'm no gossip."

"I need to know everything you know about Lord Preston and his family."

"Then get yourself comfy," she said. "This will open your eyes."

"Angela Preston, the first Lady of the Manor. She was lovely, very kind and was liked by the whole village. She organised all the village events from the annual apple pie fare to the children's pony trekking weekends around the Manor estate."

"What happened to her?" asked Todd.

"She was found dead in her bed, forty-six years old. She just died in her sleep. The village doctor put it down to heart failure, but then he was also Lord Preston's first cousin. It didn't wash with the villagers, but what could they do? Most of the village depended back then on the Manor estates for their jobs. That was many years ago."

"What about his two sons, Robert and Edward?"

"Oh, they aren't his blood," said Mrs Bruce. "Lady Angela couldn't have children. They adopted the two boys; they say they are twins but I can't see any resemblance. They were adopted at about the age of six or seven. His lordship packed them off to boarding school first chance he got. I think it was Lady Angela who wanted them. They did quite well, by all accounts."

"What do you know about the Preston treasure?"

Mrs Bruce laughed. "Well," she mused, "if there is one, it better be a big one. It will take a fortune to put the Manor back in good repair, and if you ask me, those two boys are more trouble than they are worth."

"I've already had a run in with Robert Preston. Unsavoury character," said Todd.

"You watch yourself with him," she said. "He's trouble."

"Is that all you know about the Preston treasure?"

"I can only tell you about the rumours," said Mrs Bruce. "It's supposed to be a box full of gold and jewel encrusted artefacts, church property from the days of the reformation."

"Is it true?" asked Todd.

"I don't know," she replied. "But it makes for a good story. If it is true, I wouldn't put it past the two boys to be searching for it."

"Okay," said Todd. "Thank you. You really are a mine of information," he smiled. "I'll know where to come next time I need a case solving!"

"You're very welcome," said Mrs Bruce. "So, what time are they expecting you tonight?"

"Seven on the button," he replied.

CHAPTER 7

He made his way back to Findlay's office. He was almost there when he saw the Inspector walking down Cockington lane towards the Drum.

Todd looked at his watch. "Eleven fifty-five in the morning? A bit early even for me," he mused.

Well, I never, he thought, *the doors don't open until twelve, and he doesn't even drink. Where on earth is he going?*

His curiosity got the better of him and he made his way down to the Drum. He was halfway down the lane when a car passed him with the coroner in the driver's seat.

Todd raised his eyebrows. "Surely not?" he said.

He picked up the pace and was soon crossing the car park of the Drum. The coroner's car and their police car were the only vehicles there. Todd walked over to one of the lounge windows just in time to see Findlay and the coroner sit down in one of the booths.

"Well, I never," he said under his breath, "he is a dark horse."

Todd decided to go back to the office and wait for Findlay to arrive. See if he mentioned his secret liaison.

"So," said Findlay, "what have you got for me?"

Beth shook her head. "This is a new one on me," she said. "Have you ever heard of a poison called Aconitum?"

"Pardon?" said Findlay.

"It's better known as Wolfsbane," she said. "It's uncommon, but does grow in damp heavily wooded areas around the country. It's a highly toxic plant. The interesting thing is," she said, "it wasn't ingested. It entered her body through the skin; to be precise through her hands."

Findlay sat mesmerised. "Unbelievable," he said. "How could that happen?"

"It couldn't," said Beth. "It was a deliberate act. Whoever did it, knew what they were doing."

Findlay sat bolt upright. "How on earth would she get it on her hands?"

"That's for you to work out, you're the detective. Now, what about that lunch you promised me?"

The afternoon passed quickly as they reminisced about their youth and the times they had.

Findlay looked at his watch. "Oh, my!" he exclaimed, "is that the time? I'm afraid I will have to love you and leave you," he said.

"That was an unfortunate turn of phrase," said Beth.

Findlay smiled, "It was, wasn't it? Sorry. And thanks again for getting the report out so quickly. I'll see you again, I have no doubt." He grabbed his hat and coat. Smiled at her and made his way to the exit.

It didn't take him long to reach his office where a not so happy Todd was sitting waiting.

"Ah," said Findlay, "Sergeant Todd."

"Good afternoon, sir. Have you been anywhere interesting?" said Todd.

"Interesting Sergeant? I wouldn't say so. Why do you ask?"

"No reason," said Todd.

Findlay looked at him inquisitively. "Sergeant, why do I get the feeling there's something you're not telling me?"

"It's nothing, sir. Really!"

"So, Sergeant, how did you get on with your search for the local know it all?"

"I found her, sir."

"So who might it be?"

"Actually, it's Mrs Bruce, my landlady."

Findlay's eyes opened wide. "Mrs Bruce?" he repeated. "I would take it as a personal favour if you didn't mention to her that I called her the local know it all. I once saw the village postman get on her wrong side; it was not pretty. Poor man was never the same."

"It will be our secret," said Todd.

Findlay settled into his leather chair. "Right", he said, "what did she know?"

"Well, sir, she doesn't think a lot of the Prestons. She warned me to keep an eye on the two boys. Did you know," said Todd, "they are adopted, both of them? Mrs Bruce said they are supposed to be twins. She doesn't think they are."

"She told me about a treasure supposedly hidden up at Chelston Manor."

Findlay smiled. "All these old estates have stories like that, Sergeant. If it's not treasure, it's ghosts or headless horse riders. I wouldn't think too much of it if I were you."

Todd nodded in agreement. "She also told me about Lady Angela Preston."

"Yes," said Findlay. "I remember that case, very strange. I think we need another chat with his Lordship and his two boys. Lady Victoria said she would look up the details of the deceased, her family have yet to be informed."

CHAPTER 8

Findlay and Todd made their way to Preston Manor.

"It's strange."

"What's that sir?" said Todd.

"It seems she was poisoned, but through the skin. I had lunch with Beth Middleton this afternoon. She rushed the toxicology report through as a favour. Least I could do was buy her a ploughman's lunch at the Drum."

"Oh," said Todd. "So that's what you were doing."

"I beg your pardon?" said Findlay. "What exactly do you mean, 'so that's what you were doing.'"

"Nothing sir, I saw you go into the Drum. I just wondered why."

"You'll have to do better than that Sergeant, explain yourself."

Todd turned his head and looked out of the window.

"Well?" said Findlay. "I'm waiting."

Todd turned to face him. "I'm sorry," he said. "It's just that you and the coroner do have history. You didn't mention to me that you were meeting her. I'm afraid I jumped to the wrong conclusion. I apologise."

Findlay said nothing, he just drove.

Suddenly, he pulled into a clearing and stopped. He turned to Todd.

"Yes, Sergeant, we do have history. It was over thirty years ago. There is nothing, absolutely, positively, nothing that would make me betray my wife. Is that clear?"

"Yes sir," said Todd. "I was wrong."

"Yes, Sergeant, you were. "

"It's just that I look on Mrs Findlay as the mum I never knew. As you know, mine died when I was a baby. I should have known better," said Todd. "I'm sorry."

"Right," said Findlay. "Let's say no more about it."

He restarted his old Volvo and continued up towards the Manor.

As they approached the main gate, they could see a figure standing in the driveway. It was Edward Preston. He just stood there and had no intention of moving. Findlay had no alternative but to stop. He turned off his engine, and both men climbed out.

"You must be Edward Preston?" said Todd.

"Yes, that would be me," the man replied. "And you look like the police."

"You're very astute, sir. This is Sergeant Todd and my name is Findlay. Can we have a word?"

"Do I have a choice?" said Preston. "Very well, Inspector, what is it you want to know?"

"You are aware the body of Hannah Winton was found in one of your garages?"

"Of course I'm aware. My father is devastated. If only I hadn't given her the car keys."

"Car keys?" said Todd.

"Yes. She said she had some errands to run in the village, then she was popping into town. She always cycled, but I told her to take the car."

Findlay stood motionless. "Right," he said. "That will be all for now. Thank you"

"Come along, Sergeant."

Findlay quickly made his way back to the car, with Todd following.

"Is everything alright sir?"

"Yes Sergeant. I think it is."

CHAPTER 9

F indlay made his way down Cockington Lane and headed for Torquay town.

"Can I ask where we are going, sir?" said Todd.

"Coroner's office, dear boy. I think I may just have solved a major problem."

They arrived at the coroner's office in Fleet Street, parked the car, and headed straight for Beth Middleton's room. Findlay pushed on her office door and went straight in.

Beth was sitting at her desk. "Come in, why don't you," she said sarcastically. "He doesn't see me for thirty years, now he can't bear to be away from me," she smiled.

"So, who is this?" she asked, looking at Todd.

"This is my sergeant, Allan Todd," he said quickly. "Beth, you said the poison was introduced through the skin?"

"Yes, it was," she said.

"If the poison was rubbed onto, say, leather, and she touched it, would that be enough to poison her?"

"If it was continuous contact, or rubbed in," she said. "Yes, probably. It's a powerful toxin. Why?"

"The steering wheel of the Rolls has a leather cover on it. I think somebody smeared it in the   poison. When she borrowed the car, it got onto her skin."

"But sir, that must mean she wasn't the target. She just happened to use the car," said Todd.

"That's right, Sergeant. I think the target was the only other person likely to drive the car. Lord Preston."

"When you saw the car being driven erratically, she must have been driving it, and she was trying to get back to Chelston Manor. Somebody staged the rest to make it look like suicide. It was probably whoever set the poison trap on the steering wheel."

"Who around here would know about poison? Let alone work out how to get it onto a person's skin," said Todd.

"A very determined, very sick mind, Sergeant."

"What do we do now, sir?" said Todd.

"Well, it's getting late, and you're coming to our house for dinner."

"Yes sir, I've told Mrs Bruce."

"What did she say?" asked Findlay.

"Not much sir, she just kind of grunted and said to have a nice time."

"Good," said Findlay. "Right Sergeant, see you at seven. On the dot, remember. Tomorrow is another day. Our first stop tomorrow will be Chelston Manor. His Lordship needs to know what we have found."

Findlay made his way home. On his arrival, he saw Mrs Findlay in the kitchen window. *Cooking a meal for the love birds, no doubt*, he thought. He parked his car and walked up the dimly lit path to the front door.

He no sooner put his key in, and a voice said excitedly, "Good Evening, Inspector!"

Findlay nearly jumped out of his skin. "For goodness sake!" shouted Findlay. "What is it with you people? That's the second time today I've come close to a heart attack."

"Sally," he said. "What are you doing here? Dinner isn't until seven. It's only five thirty."

"I didn't want to be late," she said. "It's very important for me to make a good impression on Allan."

Findlay shook his head. "Sally," he said, "you look lovely. I'm sure Allan will be most impressed."

"I haven't got ready yet," she replied.

"Oh," said Findlay. "May I suggest you go home and relax for an hour or so, then come back? You don't want to appear too keen, do you? You don't want to frighten him off."

Sally agreed and said she would come back in an hour.

Findlay watched her as she disappeared down the path into the night. He shook his head. "I hope my sergeant appreciates this," he mumbled.

He pushed open the front door and walked in. The smell of burning wood from the fire and the chicken Mrs Findlay was cooking reminded him of Christmas. "Hello darling," he shouted.

"Hi," she replied. "You go and sit down. I'll be through in a moment or two."

Findlay put his slippers on, which were warming in front of the open fire. He picked up the Cockington News and relaxed into his favourite leather armchair.

Mrs Findlay came in. She leaned over and gave him a kiss on the cheek.

"My, my," said Findlay. "To what do I owe that pleasure?"

She smiled. "Nothing," she said. "I just wanted you to know I love you."

Findlay smiled back. "And I love you as well, my sweet."

He folded his newspaper and placed it on the little table at the side of his chair.

He looked over the top of his black-rimmed glasses. "Go on then," he said. "What is it?"

"Well, there is just one thing, darling. I tried to book a table at our favourite restaurant, the Torbay View, but I'm afraid they were fully booked."

"Oh," said Findlay. "Well, don't worry dear, that chicken smells delicious," he replied.

"No," she said. "That's for Allan and Sally. I've booked us into the Grand Hotel, seven-thirty."

Findlay sat and stared. "The Grand?" he said.

"Yes dear. Seven-thirty, so don't leave it too late to get dressed."

With that, she disappeared back into the kitchen.

Findlay shook his head. "The Grand," he whispered. "That's going to cost me. I hope this is all worth it Sergeant, you're going to owe me for this," he continued under his breath.

CHAPTER 10

It was exactly seven when Findlay's front doorbell began ringing. He opened the door and there stood Allan Todd.

"Sergeant," he said. "Please come in."

"Thank you," said Todd. "And seeing as we are not on duty, could you please call me Allan?"

Findlay looked him in the eye for a few seconds, then said. "Come in, Allan," and smiled.

He took him through to the lounge with its roaring open fire. "I will just be a moment, Serg... Sorry, I mean, Allan."

He had just closed the door to the lounge when there was a faint knock on the front door.

He opened it and there stood Sally, looking radiant. She had obviously pulled out all the stops; she looked like she had stepped off the set of a movie.

"Oh my!" said Findlay. "Sally, you look beautiful."

"Thank you," she said, beaming.

"Do please come in."

He ushered her in and closed the door behind her. Showing her to the kitchen where Mrs Findlay had set the scene. The large oak kitchen table was laid with a white lace cloth and crisp white cotton serviettes. She had even brought out their best silverware and crystal wine glasses, and a log fire burned in the hearth.

"Oh, Mrs F!" gasped Sally. "It's lovely! Thank you so much."

"It's our pleasure, isn't it, dear?"

Findlay cleared his throat. "Yes, yes, indeed it is. I will go and get Allan," he said.

He made his way to the front room and opened the door. Todd stood warming his rear end against the open fire.

"Right Allan," said Findlay. "This way."

"Thank you, sir. It's so nice of you and Mrs Findlay to invite me."

"Really?" said Findlay. "We will see!" he said with a chuckle.

He opened the door to the kitchen. "After you, Allan," said Findlay.

The pair walked in; Todd stopped dead in his tracks.

Sally was standing at the head of the table. The outside garden light shining behind her gave her the look of an angel in her white chiffon dress.

She stood and smiled. Todd was riveted to the spot.

"I have a confession to make," said Findlay. "Mrs Findlay and I have done a little matchmaking. A meal has been prepared for you both. There's a bottle of wine on the table, the house is yours. Just don't burn it down!"

"Oh," said Mrs Findlay. "Seeing as you didn't know anything about tonight, Allan; I got these for you to give Sally," and handed him a bouquet of red roses.

"And now," said Mrs Findlay, "we will be on our way. Enjoy the meal, and Allan.... smile!"

At that, the front door clicked shut, and they were gone.

"Well Sal, this is a turn up for the books, I had no idea."

Sally smiled. "Would you have come if you had known?"

"I'll be honest, Sal, probably not. Not because I don't want to spend time with you. I do." He added hastily. "I'm just not very good with girls, erm, I mean, women."

"Well, Mrs F has gone to a lot of trouble. The least we can do is have dinner. What do you think?"

Todd nodded and smiled. "Can't hurt, can it? And it does smell lovely. Ok," he said. "Let's get stuck in!"

To both of their surprise, they had so much in common. They even liked the same brands of tea. Todd poured the last of the wine from the bottle. "Looks like that's it," he said and poured half from his glass into hers. "I've really enjoyed myself tonight, Sal."

"So have I," she said.

"Could we do it again?" asked Todd.

"Yes," she said with a beaming smile. "I hope so, I would love to."

"I will come into the Drum sometime this week to see you, if that's okay?"

"You can't miss me," said Sally, "seeing as I work behind the bar."

"I'm just really busy with work," said Todd. "I'm trying to find out all I can about the Preston boys."

"Then look no further," she said. "I went to Cockington Primary school with them. Dad used to drop me off at the manor to play with them when I was little."

"Well, well," said Todd. "That would save me some leg work."

"I can only really tell you up to the day they went off to University. Cambridge, naturally," she said. "Edward managed about a year, but Robert did the full three years. He graduated with honours, I think."

"Oh?" said Todd. "What did he graduate as?"

"A chemist, I think. Whatever a biochemist is," she said. "He's actually quite bright."

Sally sat for a few seconds. "Be very careful if Robert is around," she said. "He's a bad one. Edward is okay, but I wouldn't fully trust either of them."

"This is going to sound really strange," said Todd. "But have you heard the rumours of the Chelston treasure?"

"Yes," said Sally. "The stories have been going around for years. It's said that when the churches were ransacked in the fifteen hundreds. All the gold and jewels held by the Catholic Church were gathered together and brought here to Cockington. Chelston Manor was built on the grounds of the old priory. The ground underneath the manor is a rabbit warren of passages and tunnels."

"How do you know all this?" asked Todd.

"I was brought up on such stories," she said. "Nobody really believes them, of course, but the old catacombs are definitely there. I guess you never know."

"That girl they found up at the manor, Hannah Winton," said Todd.

"She was in the Drum a while back. I think her and his Lordship had words. She drank a few too many gin and tonics. She was telling me that her and Robert Preston were searching the tunnels looking for clues. Poor girl, won't do her much good now, will it?"

"I wonder if his Lordship is aware that Robert is searching for the treasure?" said Todd.

"I doubt it. I doubt he believes it ever existed. If he did, he would probably have found it by now," said Sally.

"You're a mine of information," said Todd.

Sally just smiled. "It's amazing what you can pick up in the local pub," she said.

"I'd better get you home," said Todd. "Mr and Mrs Findlay will be back soon."

Todd picked up the silk shawl she was wearing and placed it around her shoulders.

"Thank you," she said.

The two stood in front of the still roaring fire and looked into each other's eyes. Sally made the first move as she raised her hand and placed it on his cheek. She slowly stood on tiptoes and their lips touched. It was then that Todd felt this overwhelming feeling of clarity. He knew at that moment he was falling in love.

He didn't know whether he should be ridiculously happy, or simply terrified. It had never happened to him before, and he wasn't sure what he was supposed to do. For a moment, he was stuck for words.

Sally stood and gazed at him. "We'd better go," she said.

"Yes, of course," said Todd quickly. He held the door open for her and they stepped into the cool air of the autumn night as Todd closed the door behind them.

CHAPTER 11

T he following morning, Todd arrived at the office. "Late, as always," said Findlay.

"Sorry sir," said Todd.

"Well, Sergeant? How did your evening go?"

"It went well, sir. Thank you."

Findlay sat in silence, waiting. "Well?" he said. "Is that it? Did you talk? Did you hit it off? Come along, Sergeant I need more than 'it went well!' It cost me a week's wages at the Grand. Mrs F will want to know all the details, so let's have them."

"It went very, very, well, sir. Yes, in fact, I think it went too well."

"I'm confused," said Findlay. "What do you mean, too well? I hope you didn't disgrace yourself, Sergeant?"

"Oh, my god no sir. Nothing like that, I wouldn't!"

"I just meant," he sat quietly for a few seconds. Then said, "I think I'm in love with her, sir."

"Well, well," said Findlay. "That poor girl! Let's hope she doesn't blame Mrs Findlay and I." He smiled.

"Does she feel the same way?"

"I don't know, sir. I honestly don't know. I hope so."

Findlay thought for a second. "I think there's a good chance she does, Sergeant. I'll have a word with Mrs Findlay, she will find out for you. She's good at getting that kind of information from people. I think it's a gift she has."

"Now, Sergeant, back to business. Have you managed to find out anything about the two Preston boys?"

"Quite a lot," said Todd. "It seems Sally is a childhood friend of both of them. She used to go to the Manor to play when she was little. She said her dad used to drop her off and she would spend the day playing with the two boys."

"Did Sally mention what happened to Mardie's parents?" asked Findlay.

"No sir, she didn't."

"I see," said Findlay.

"Why do I get the impression I'm missing something?" replied Todd.

"It seems they were both killed in a car accident when Mardie was little. Seems the brakes on their car failed on the way down Vicarage Hill. They hit the church wall at the bottom and were both killed instantly. Tragic. Then Lord Preston allowed an aunt of Mardie to live in the gatehouse and bring her up. She died when Mardie was a teenager. He let her stay on as the gardener. She had learned the ropes from her father. She was doing okay until Lord Preston gave the estate cottages to his sons to manage."

"So that's why she lives in a hut on the grounds?"

"Yes, Sergeant, that's exactly it."

"One interesting thing I found out, sir; it seems Robert Preston graduated from Cambridge with honours, as, get this sir, a chemist."

"Really?" said Findlay. "Well, that would certainly answer the question of who would know about obscure poisons and how to administer them. He would presumably stand to benefit from the death of Lord Preston as the eldest son."

"What about Edward Preston?" asked Todd.

"In normal circumstances he would only inherit if both father and brother are dead," said Findlay. "It would all depend on Lord Preston's last will and testament, who the beneficiaries are, and do they know? From what I can gather, the first Lady Preston adopted the two boys. The question is, are they mentioned in the will as they are not his blood?"

"We need to get a look at his last will, Sergeant."

"We could just ask Lord Preston," said Todd.

Findlay smiled. "Do you think he would honestly show us his will? I think this being in love is playing tricks with your brain."

"Very well," said Findlay. "I will go to the courthouse and see if I can get a court order to look at the will. I want you to speak with Robert Preston, see what kind of relationship he and the deceased had."

"Yes sir," said Todd.

"And I'll meet you back here at two."

Meanwhile, at the Preston estate, Mardie was in the driveway clearing weeds. She was happily humming a tune and getting on with her work, when suddenly behind her she heard

"What are you doing, you fool?" in a very loud voice which made her jump.

It was Robert Preston. He walked around her, saying nothing. Then picked up the bucket Mardie had been putting the weeds in.

"Where did you get this bucket?" he asked.

"From the stable block," she replied.

"You know stable buckets are for the stables, not the garden!" He grinned and tipped the bucket upside down, spilling the dead weeds back onto the driveway. He then threw the bucket onto the lawn.

"I'm sorry," said Mardie.

"Don't be sorry, you idiot, just get it right. Now look what you made me do!" he growled, looking down at the mess on the driveway. "How stupid can you be? Now go and get a bucket from the greenhouse and pick up this mess before I report you to my father for incompetence!"

Mardie just whispered, "Yes sir."

She walked over and picked up the bucket. She kept her eyes to the ground and made her way across the lawn towards the stables.

"Don't walk on the lawns!" he shouted. "Use the path, you idiot."

Mardie was used to his insults. She had lived her whole life being treated badly by the two boys, but more so by Robert. The only one who was nice to her was Lord Preston, but she so rarely saw him. She was afraid to answer back in case she lost her job. It might not be a good job or the best place to live, but it was better than living on the streets.

Mardie arrived at the stable block and started her search for a bucket. Suddenly, a voice said,

"Why do you allow him to speak to you like that?"

It was Lady Victoria. "You don't have to put up with that kind of treatment, especially from a bloated toad like Robert Preston."

"I don't wants to cause any trouble," she said. "I just wants a quiet life to care for my plants and trees, that's all I wants.
"

"There are things you don't know, Mardie," said Lady Victoria. "Things that have been kept secret from you. Things I've found out."

"Things like what?" said Mardie.

She didn't answer.

"Mardie," she said, "what a lovely bracelet. Where did you get it?"

"I found it," she replied.

"May I have a look at it?" she said.

Mardie unclipped it and handed it to Lady Victoria.

She laid it on her palm and looked closely at it. "That's old, and it's gold," she thought.

"When you say you found it, Mardie, exactly where did you find it?"

She didn't answer. She just stared at the ground.

"I didn't steal it," she said.

"Of course not," said Lady Victoria. "But where did you find it? It's okay, you can tell me. It will be our secret."

She thought for a second, then said, "In them tunnels, there be some lovely things down there to find."

Lady Victoria stared at her. "Alright Mardie," she said. "It's our secret. Maybe you could show me where the tunnel is? But not today." She handed Mardie a bucket. "You'd better keep Robert happy. Go and clear your driveway, and Mardie, maybe you should put your bracelet in your pocket. You wouldn't want Robert to see it and take it away from you, would you?"

Mardie shook her head, put the bracelet in her pocket, took the bucket and made her way back to the mess Robert had made.

Lady Victoria slowly shook her head as she watched her walking up the driveway. "Poor girl," she muttered, "if only you knew."

Lady Victoria was about to walk back to the Annex when a car pulled into the driveway. It was Todd.

"Well," she said, "if it isn't the adorable Sergeant Todd. Is this a business call Sergeant or have you made a special trip to see me?" she smiled.

"No, no," protested Todd, flustered. "It's business. I need to speak to the boys; Robert Preston preferably."

"Why Sergeant," she said, "I'm hurt."

Todd could feel his face turning red, so he turned quickly, and walked towards the Manor.

"If you would like a chat, you know where to find me!" she shouted after him and smiled.

Todd didn't reply. He saw Mardie working on the flower borders, so walked over to her.

"Good morning," he said cheerfully.

"Morning," she said, and carried on turning the soil.

"I'm here to see Robert or Edward. Would you know where I can find them?"

"No," she said abruptly, "and I don't care. He did it, you know?"

"Who did what?" asked Todd.

She didn't answer.

"Mardie?" he said again. "Who did what?"

CHAPTER 12

S uddenly, a voice came from across the lawn.

"Back again?" it said. "What do you want this time? And leave the servants alone. Especially this one," he said, looking at Mardie. It was Robert Preston.

"I need a chat," said Todd.

"How exciting," he said. "I can't wait."

He turned and walked towards the Manor. "Well?" he shouted. "Are you coming or what?"

Todd followed him back to the tradesmen's door at the side of the Manor. Robert pushed it open and went inside. Todd followed.

"Make it quick," he said. "I have important things to do, unlike you."

Todd took a deep breath. *Horrid little man,* he thought to himself.

"How well did you know Hannah, your father's secretary?" said Todd.

Robert smiled. "And why would you want to know that?"

"Please just answer the question, sir. How well did you know her?"

"She worked for my father," he said.

"I have it on good authority, sir, that you and she were very close."

"If you mean, was I sleeping with her? No, I was not! Don't believe everything you hear," he said, "and what gives you the right to question me like this? Do you know who I am? One day all this will be mine and the likes of you will be bowing down to me. Now, who told you I was sleeping with her?" he snarled. "Was it that fool of a gardener? You do know she hates me, don't you?"

Todd glared at him. "What exactly does that mean? 'Hates you,'" asked Todd.

"I think you know what I mean," said Robert. "I'll be having a stern word with her later."

"No sir, you won't!" Todd reached over and pushed the kitchen door closed.

"What do you think you're doing?" said Robert.

Todd stood for a few seconds, staring at him.

Then, in a calm, quiet tone of voice, Todd said, "I love my job. I love helping people. I love it when a problem gets solved. Unfortunately, it also means I occasionally come across totally unscrupulous, mean mouthed, little scumbags like you! So, I'm going to say this once. If I hear you've been mistreating that young girl, or if it comes to that, if you speak to me ever again the way you have done this afternoon. I will come back. I will then drag your lifeless body into the woods and I will leave you there for the wildlife to feed upon. Do I make myself clear?"

Robert stood open-mouthed. He couldn't believe the way Todd had spoken to him.

Todd said again, "Well, sir? Do I make myself clear?"

"Yes," said Robert, "Quite clear."

"Good," said Todd. "Now, sir, I may need to speak to you again. Thank you for your time. Don't forget what I said. It would not be a good idea to ignore me."

At that, Todd unlocked the door and left, slamming it hard behind him.

He was walking back to his car, still shaking with anger, when he saw Inspector Findlay coming up the drive. Findlay pulled up and parked next to the police car.

"Got it," he said, waving a court order out of the window.

"Got what?" said Todd. "Oh, the court order."

"Yes sergeant. Now we can see who stands to gain most from his Lordship's demise."

They made their way up the marble steps to the front door. Todd was about to bang on the oak doors when Findlay raised his hand and stopped him.

"Allow me, Sergeant," he reached out and gave the doors a hefty shove. They slowly swung open. Findlay smiled. As they stepped inside, Simonds appeared at the top of the sweeping staircase.

"Who the hell?" he shouted.

Findlay spoke out before he could complete his sentence, "You really do need to get your front door fixed sir. Anybody could just walk in. "

"Now, my good man, be kind enough to tell his lordship I need to speak to him. And before you ask, I have a court order for him."

"You know where the study is," said Simonds. "Find your own way," he said sullenly.

"Thank you," said Findlay.

He and Todd made their way up the white marble staircase.

"It's creepy, isn't it, sir?"

"What is Sergeant?"

"All these paintings. It's like they are watching us."

"Maybe they are, Sergeant. Maybe they are."

They reached the study. Findlay knocked on the door, no answer.

He knocked again, still no answer.

Todd gently pushed on the door and it slowly opened. The two men entered.

Lord Preston was sitting in a leather fireside armchair in front of a roaring open fire, drink in hand.

"Good afternoon, sir," said Findlay. "We have some information for you regarding the death of Hannah Winton."

Lord Preston did not answer him.

Findlay held out the court order. "I also have some paperwork for you, sir."

Preston still did not answer him.

Todd walked slowly around the chair and stood between Lord Preston and the fire. He bent over and touched Lord Preston's hand. His whisky glass crashed to the floor.

Findlay checked for a pulse. Todd listened for a sign of life. Nothing.

"Damn, I think he's dead," said Findlay.

They stood back and looked at each other.

"Oh my god!" said Todd.

"Right, Sergeant, this is now a possible crime scene. I need you to find a phone and wait for emergency services and contact the coroner. I need Beth up here as soon as possible."

Todd was about to leave when he noticed a pill bottle laying under Lord Preston's chair.

"Sir," said Todd. He bent down to pick it up.

"Leave it, Sergeant! Don't touch it. Two deaths in three days in the same household. It doesn't take a genius to work it out. Go and make those calls, and find out where Robert Preston and Lady Victoria are. And if you see Simonds the valet, send him up."

Todd went to call for the emergency services. He was halfway down the main staircase when Simonds appeared at the bottom.

Todd stopped. "Stay where you are," he said.

Simonds shook his head, "Now what is it? Forgotten where the front door is, have you?"

"I'm afraid it's his Lordship. He's dead," said Todd.

Simonds looked at him with disbelief. "What do you mean, dead?" he replied. "I took him his morning tea not an hour ago."

He was quiet for a minute, then said, "How did he die?"

"No idea yet," said Todd.

"Where is he?" asked Simonds.

"He's in the study," said Todd. "Inspector Findlay is with him."

"Then I must go up!" said Simonds.

"No," said Todd. "You can't go in there, not yet. I'm going for an ambulance, you stay here."

"Oh my god," said Simonds. "What about Edward, his son? Young Edward is arriving this afternoon from Exeter. Oh dear! What am I going to say to him?"

Todd didn't answer. He just shrugged his shoulders.

Todd quickly left and made his way over to the Annex. He knew Lady Victoria had a phone.

The door to the Annex was open. Todd knocked and shouted, "Hello?"

"Hello?" he said again. "Is anyone there?"

"Well, well, Sergeant," said Lady Victoria with a smile. "What a pleasant surprise, and so soon."

"This isn't a social call," said Todd. "May I come in?"

"Of course, Sergeant. Whatever is wrong?"

"You may need to sit down," said Todd.

Lady Victoria sat down. "Sergeant, you're frightening me. What's wrong?"

Todd sat next to her. "It's Lord Preston, I'm sorry, but he is dead."

For a second, she stared at him. "Don't be ridiculous," she said. "How can he be dead? You're mistaken, surely?"

"I'm afraid not," said Todd. "Inspector Findlay and I found him in his study."

"How?" she asked.

"We don't know yet. May I use your phone? I have to call for help?"

She nodded.

Todd made the necessary calls and returned to the lounge. Lady Victoria was still sitting on the settee in a state of shock.

Todd sat down next to her again. "Are you alright?" he asked.

"Yes, I think so. I just can't believe it. What is happening? First Hannah, now David. What on earth is happening?"

"We have no idea yet," said Todd, "but I don't think it's safe for you to stay here. Is there anyone you can stay with for a couple of days? A relative or friends?"

She sat for a few seconds. "I'm going nowhere," she said. "Not until I know what is going on."

"If that's what you want," said Todd. "I must go and wait for the emergency services to arrive. I think locking your doors would be a good idea, just for now."

Lady Victoria grabbed Todd's hand. "Please don't leave me alone!" she begged.

Todd was taken by surprise. "But I have to wait for the ambulance," he said.

"Please Sergeant! Allan, isn't it?"

"Yes," he replied.

"Please Allan, stay with me. Just until help gets here!"

"Very well," he said. "Just for a while."

"It's awful," she said. "Why are these horrible things happening? Do you think somebody could be doing it?"

"I don't know," said Todd. "It's all very strange. These are the kind of things that happen in the cities, like Plymouth or Exeter, not sleepy Cockington Village."

They sat quietly for a few seconds. Lady Victoria suddenly leaned in towards him, and with no warning, kissed him on the lips.

Todd didn't know how to respond. He just stared at her. Then she leaned forward again.

Todd jumped up. "I'm sorry," he said. "You're a beautiful woman, but I already have somebody, or at least I think I do."

"No Allan, it was me who kissed you. I'm the one who is sorry. I don't know why I did that. It's just shock, I think. Please forgive me!"

Todd nodded. "We will say no more," he said.

They stood in awkward silence for what seemed a lifetime.

"I'd better go," said Todd.

"Allan?" she said. "I am truly sorry."

Todd smiled and left.

She stood at the window and watched as he made his way to the main gates to await the coroner.

She was about to walk away when she spotted Mardie crossing the stable yard. She quickly put on her jacket and hurried to try and catch up with her. "Mardie!" she shouted.

Mardie stopped and turned around. "Lady Victoria, what can I do for you?"

"I wondered if we could have a chat?"

"A chat about what?" said Mardie.

"A chat about your mum and dad," she said.

"I don't wants to talk about them," said Mardie.

"I thought we were friends?" said Lady Victoria.

"Friends?" said Mardie.

"Yes, friends," said Lady Victoria. "I was asked to find some-thing yesterday. I was going through some old boxes in the attic. There's something you need to see," she said. "Would you come back to the Annex with me?"

"I don't understands," said Mardie.

"I know you don't. Come with me, I'll explain. Please come," she said again.

Mardie nodded and the two of them made their way back to the Annex.

CHAPTER 13

T odd and Findlay were about to show the ambulance men up to Lord Preston's study. Simonds sat in a chair by the cellar door and said nothing.

They were halfway up the staircase when Beth arrived. "Go to Devon, they said. Nothing ever happens down there, they said! Good heavens," she muttered.

"Beth, when you're finished wittering."

"I don't witter!" she replied.

"Oh yes you do," said Findlay.

She made her way up the staircase and joined them. Accompanied by the two ambulance men, they made their way to the study.

As they entered, there was a figure of a man standing over the still seated body of Lord Preston.

"Who the hell are you?" shouted Findlay, "and who let you in here?"

The figure turned around. "My name is Edward Preston. And this is, or was, my father."

"I don't give a damn who you are," said Findlay. "How the hell did you get in here? I know you didn't come up the stairs. I've been here for the last hour."

"I was raised here," he said. "I know every inch of Chelston Manor. I don't need doors and stairs. And you are?" he asked.

"My name is Findlay, Inspector Findlay, and this is Sergeant Todd. We are from Cockington police station."

"Where's my useless brother?" said Edward, "and where's the grieving widow Victoria?"

"Lady Victoria has been informed," said Todd. "We haven't as yet spoken to your brother."

"Hmm," said Edward. "He won't be far away. He never is when there's trouble. So how did my father meet his end, Inspector? Heart attack, I presume?"

"As yet, sir, that hasn't been determined."

"And that, Gentlemen, is my job," said Beth, pushing her way into the study. "When I am finished doing my job," she said angrily, "I will let you know. Now! It's like Piccadilly Station in here, everybody out except for the ambulance men."

"I don't mind saying sir, you don't seem too distressed," said Beth, "considering your father is lying or rather, sitting, dead in front of you?"

"I'm not," said Edward. "Just the opposite."

"We better go out," said Findlay, opening the study door.

When in the hallway, Findlay said, "What did you mean, just the opposite?"

"My father and I did not have a close relationship. I owed him nothing. Everything I have or have become, I owe to my adopted mother. He killed her, you know?"

"I beg your pardon?" said Findlay.

"Oh, he didn't squeeze the life out of her, but he might just as well have."

Findlay and Todd stared at each other.

"Go on," said Findlay.

"My father," he said, "he broke mum's heart when she found out about his affair, and with a servant of all people."

"Which servant was this, sir?" asked Findlay.

"The gardener's wife, she was our cook, Mrs Ellis."

"Janet Ellis?" said Findlay. "That was over twenty years ago. So, you're saying your father had an affair with Janet Ellis?"

"Yes," he replied. "Her husband Jack came looking for my father. He was going to kill him. He probably would have done if it hadn't been for Simonds. I think the old fool was actually in love with her. Can you imagine, falling for a servant, a cook at that? That's what killed my mother. She died of a broken heart; it was him who broke it. So, I have little sympathy for him."

"Well," said Findlay, "that's more information than I expected. Thank you for being so honest."

"Like I said, Inspector, I have no sympathy for him, and unlike my brother, I have nothing to hide."

"And what might your brother be hiding?" asked Todd.

Edward didn't get a chance to answer. Beth came from the study. "I'm all done, Inspector. As always, as soon as I have the results, I will be in touch."

Beth stood to one side while the ambulance men passed carrying a stretcher with the covered body of Lord Preston on it. They carefully made their way down the marble stairway. Simonds was standing at the bottom, looking ashen. He said nothing as they and Beth passed and made their way to the ambulance. He just stood and watched.

"Don't look so sad Simonds," said a voice from the top of the cellar steps. It was Robert Preston. "I've just been informed my father has passed away?"

"Yes, I'm afraid so," said Findlay.

"Then, as the eldest son, you will deal with me from now on," he said.

"Well, Inspector, we are keeping you busy are we not?" said Robert. "And look who's here, brother Edward, we haven't seen you here for quite some time!"

"Would you like tea, Inspector? I'll send my man Simonds to get it for you."

Simonds glared at him.

Robert walked around Simonds like an animal stalking its prey.

"I suppose you work for me now," he said with a smile. "You don't have to like me," he whispered in Simonds' ear, "but you do now need to respect me. If you want to keep your home and job, that is."

"Strange you should show up on the very day dear daddy passes away, brother. You do know that as the eldest son, I inherit everything?"

Edward didn't answer.

He turned to Findlay. "If you need to talk to me, Inspector, I'll be here for a while yet."

He then looked at Robert. "So, brother, you are as obnoxious as ever I see. Father's not cold yet and you are wearing his crown."

Edward shook his head and made his way upstairs.

"Nothing we can do here, Sergeant," said Findlay. "We will go back to the village and try to work out just exactly what's going on. It's even more important now that we see his Lordships will."

Meanwhile, Lady Victoria and Mardie arrived at the Annex.

"Please sit," said Victoria.

Mardie sat down.

"Have they told you about his Lordship?" she asked.

Mardie nodded.

"Who told you?" she asked.

"Simonds told me," replied Mardie.

"Very well," she said. Lady Victoria then lifted a cardboard box from under a coffee table and placed it in front of Mardie.

"I found this," she said, and opened it. She took out a stack of envelopes wrapped with a blue ribbon. Victoria removed the ribbon and opened the top letter.

"These are letters and messages passed between your mother and Lord Preston over twenty-three or more years ago. There are maybe fifty of them covering a three-year period. It seems Robert and Edward all these years were telling the truth; your mother and his Lordship were having an affair."

Mardie just sat and stared at the box.

"I know this will be difficult for you," said Victoria. "There are things you need to know. Things that have been kept from you. There is one letter here, dated October 1923. It's from your mother to Lord Preston. Mardie, I'm going to read it to you, is that alright?"

Mardie looked at her, then nodded.

Lady Victoria took the letter from its envelope, opened it and began reading.

"My darling David,

I know you said we could not be in contact with each other again and I am sorry, but I miss you. I love you so much the thought of never again being able to hold you breaks my heart.

I understand how difficult it must be for you after the death of your wife and how heartbroken the two children must be. I have no wish to make it any harder for you, but there is something you have to know, I am having a baby, it is your baby my darling.

I cannot keep this from Jack, I shall be telling him the news this very evening. He is not a violent man, but I do not know how he will react to my news, so I implore you to be careful.

I am yours always and most lovingly,

Janet."

Victoria placed the letter on the table top and pulled another envelope out of the box.

She took out its contents.

"I also found this one. It is a birth certificate for a child born 15th of April 1924. She was named Maria Diane Preston. The birth mother is registered as Janet Ellis. It's your mother, Mardie. 'Mar D' was your father's pet name for you. He knew that one day somebody would put it together. That somebody is me. Mardie, you are that child. You are Maria Diane Preston; the rightful heiress to the Preston estates and fortune."

"My husband kept this from you for nineteen years. You have been treated terribly, but all of that will now change. We must keep this from the boys. They are both dangerous and I don't know how they will react to the news that you own everything they have. Not well, I think.

"Now Mardie, your bracelet, do you have it?"

"Yes," she said.

"Is this all you have?"

"Yes," said Mardie. "I did have a ring, but I gave it to Hannah."

"What kind of a ring was it?" asked Victoria.

"T'was a big one," she said. "Pretty red, green and purple stones in it. I think maybe it was a man's ring."

She took the bracelet from her coat pocket and handed it to Lady Victoria.

She held it up to the light and smiled. "Do you remember where you found this?"

Mardie nodded.

"Will you take me there?"

"Yes," she replied.

"We can't do this alone. The boys are looking for the Preston treasure. They have been searching for years. I am going to see Inspector Findlay and Allan Todd. We will need their help," said Victoria.

CHAPTER 14

Findlay and Todd were in their office sifting through realms of paperwork, looking for that one clue that might help them make head or tail of this case.

Findlay sat back in his chair. "It's no good Sergeant, my head is swimming. Let's call it a day. Maybe tomorrow it will make sense."

He arrived home exhausted.

"Hello dear," said Mrs Findlay. "You look like you've had a day of it?"

Findlay smiled. "You could say that."

"Your slippers are warming, dear. Put them on and go and sit down. Dinner won't be long," she said. "I'll bring you a pot of tea."

Findlay put his slippers on and sat down in front of a roaring fire. He closed his eyes and tried putting the day's events in place, but he couldn't.

"Here you are dear," said Mrs Findlay. "A nice hot pot of tea always does the trick."

She sat on the arm of his chair and ran her hand across his cheek.

Findlay smiled and took hold of her hand. "All the tea in China can't compare to one touch from you, my sweet."

"So, what's wrong?" she said.

Findlay told her what had happened to Lord Preston, and how he must get down to the coroner's office first thing in the morning.

"Well," she said. "I'm shocked, that poor man and his family. It sounds to me like you need to get a look at that will. Whoever the beneficiaries are will probably be who you are looking for. Do you have anyone in mind?" she asked.

"Several, actually," he replied. "Which doesn't help me any. The valet, Simonds. He's been with the family for decades, but there's something about him. I wouldn't trust him. Then there is Robert Preston, the eldest of the two boys, he's a real nasty piece of work. If it turns out Lord Preston was murdered, would I look at Robert? The answer is yes. I wouldn't put anything past him. Lady Victoria, a woman scorned, do I think she's capable of murder? No, I would say not, but I'm not ruling her out. Then there is Edward Preston, the youngest of the two boys born just an hour after Robert. I don't know, I simply don't know. In a way, they all stand to gain from his death, but until I can get sight of the Will, I won't know."

Mrs Findlay leaned forward and gave him a kiss. "You'll sort it out, dear. You always do."

Findlay raised his eyebrows. "Maybe," he said. "Maybe."

Findlay and his wife had just finished their evening meal. He was standing at the kitchen sink washing the dishes, and up to his elbows in soapsuds when there was a knock at the front door.

"What time is it, dear?"

"It's eight fifty-five," she replied. "Who on earth would be calling at this time?"

Findlay went into the lounge and pulled back the heavy draped curtains to see who was there.

"Good heavens," said Findlay.

"Who is it dear?" asked Mrs Findlay.

"It's Lady Victoria."

Findlay hurried to the front door and opened it. "Lady Victoria, please come in." He closed the door behind her. "This is an unexpected visit."

"I am sorry to come to your home, but there are things you need to know."

Findlay showed her into the best room with the large open fire and the brown leather furnishings. Mrs Findlay was very proud of her best room, although not many had visited her to see it.

"This is Mrs Findlay," he said.

"Lady Victoria," said Mrs Findlay. "What a pleasure. I'll fetch a pot of fresh tea, shall I?"

At that, she disappeared into the kitchen.

"First things first," she said. "Please, just call me Victoria. I've never liked being known as a title."

"Of course," he said. "Please sit down."

She opened her bag and took out the envelopes she had shown Mardie.

"Please read these," she said, and handed him the letter sent to Lord Preston from Janet Ellis.

Findlay read it, then sat back in his chair.

"Now this one," she said, and handed him the birth certificate.

Findlay read it. Then he said, "Good god. What a Pandora's box is about to be opened!"

"I have spoken to Mardie," she said. "I don't know if she fully understands what is happening, or who she really is."

She then reached into her pocket and pulled out the gold bracelet. "Look at this," she said, handing it to Findlay.

Findlay sat and stared at it. "Is this solid gold?"

"Yes, it is. Mardie found it in the tunnels that run under the Manor. She also said there was a large ring with different coloured stones; obviously precious stones. She gave it to Hannah. She said there's lots of things to be found down there."

Findlay got up from his chair and stood in front of the fire, still looking at the bracelet.

"Do you realise," he said, "this could be the Preston Manor treasure?"

"There's no could about it, Inspector. It is the treasure! Mardie said she would show us where it is. I can only imagine what Robert and Edward would do to get their hands on this. That's why I'm here. I will need yours and Allan's help."

"Allan?" said Findlay.

"Yes," she said. "That is Sergeant Todd's first name, isn't it?"

"Yes," said Findlay, "I'm just not used to hearing it," he said, handing her back the bracelet.

"You must keep this to yourself," he said. "Nobody at the manor must find out. Not yet."

Findlay arranged to meet her the next day at the Annex with Allan Todd. "Be sure Mardie is with you," he said. "I have to call in to see Beth, the coroner, first thing. So, I will be here around nine. We will see what she has to show us, then it will be time to tell the Preston boys the bad news."

The best room door opened and Mrs Findlay entered carrying a large wooden tray with a pot of tea and biscuits and, of course, her best China. She placed the tray on the table and sat down next to Findlay.

"How are you holding up through all of this?" asked Mrs Findlay.

"I am holding up well. Thank you for asking. You're the only one who has."

Mrs Findlay picked up the tea pot and poured.

"Milk?" she asked.

"No thank you," said Victoria.

They sat for a few seconds, sipping their tea.

"Millions," said Findlay.

"Pardon dear?" said Mrs Findlay.

"Yes, millions. The manor, the estates, the properties, and now a possible fortune in gold and jewels. Young Mardie will be worth millions."

"How do you feel about that, Victoria?" asked Findlay.

"If I said I didn't care, I would be telling you lies," she said. "But Mardie is the hereditary Lady of Preston Manor. She has to claim her birthright, but I am afraid of what Robert will do when he finds out. When I found these documents, the solicitor's wax seal was already broken. I don't think I was the first to read it."

"Do you think Robert or Edward already know?" asked Findlay.

"I don't think so," replied Victoria. "If it was them, surely they would have destroyed the evidence?"

"Maybe it was Lord Preston?" said Findlay.

"Why would he? He already knew what they said. No," said Victoria, "I don't know who it was, but someone broke that seal."

CHAPTER 15

The next morning, Findlay was up and about early. He sat at the kitchen table, running over everything in his head. He finished his tea and toast, put on his top coat, gloves and hat, and made his way down to his office in Cockington Village.

As he arrived, he was surprised to see Beth standing at the front door. "Beth," he said, "what a pleasure, and so early."

"I've had the results on the post mortem on Lord Preston. It's not good news," she said.

Findlay opened the large brown envelope, removed its contents, and read it.

"So, you are saying he was murdered, and it's the same poison?"

Beth nodded. "In a nutshell, yes, but not the same means of delivery."

"Whoever is doing this is a highly skilled botanist. The roots are where the highest level of poison is found, although it is still found in the flower," she said. "If the victim had any cuts on the hands, for instance, it would enter the bloodstream and cause arrhythmia, paralysis, and eventually death. It would also be very, very quick. Lord Preston had a cut to his palm, so he would have had no chance of calling for help, or at least, it's unlikely," said Beth.

"So, if, for instance, the intended victim was sat in front of a fire with a glass in his hand and that glass had been coated in the poison?" said Findlay.

"And you had an open wound on your hand," said Beth, "then you are going to die."

"Good god!" exclaimed Findlay. "So, our killer is in the manor."

"I've done all I can do," said Beth. "Good luck, Inspector." And she walked towards her car.

Findlay stood with his key in the lock and watched her cross the village square. She suddenly stopped and turned. "I will be in the Drum at eight," she shouted and disappeared around the corner.

Findlay slowly shook his head and turned the key. He was about to push on the door when he saw Todd walking down the hill from home.

Findlay smiled at Sergeant Todd, who had his hands in his pockets whistling and not a care in the world.

"You need to go home, Sergeant. We are going treasure hunting! Change your clothes and be back here in half an hour." And he closed the door behind him.

Todd stood still. "Treasure hunting?" he mumbled. "Change my clothes? Okay," he thought. He turned around and made his way back home.

Knowing the trouble he would be in if he was late, Todd was back in less than half that time.

"Right, Sergeant, we are going to the Manor. I'll fill you in on the way."

The two men made their way towards Chelston Manor, and Inspector Findlay told Todd about the visit from Lady Victoria and the report from Beth.

"So," said Todd, "we are going treasure hunting? How exciting."

"No, Sergeant, you are the one going treasure hunting. I am going for a chat with Robert Preston and Simonds. Lady Victoria is meeting you at the Annex with Mardie. Just go along and see what's in the tunnels."

Todd made his way to the Annex, while Findlay climbed the steps to the Manor. He pushed on the oak doors and they once again slowly opened. Findlay stepped inside. "There's that smell again," he muttered, "musty."

"Hello?" he shouted.

He stood very still and waited for a reply.

"Hello?" he shouted again. Still no reply.

Findlay noticed the door to the cellar was opened, he walked over and peered down into the darkness. Something was telling him to go down and have a look. Something else was telling him, *Don't be so stupid. Wait until Todd is here.*

He knew it was a mistake, but his curiosity got the better of him. He felt around on the wall for a light switch. There didn't seem to be one. He suddenly felt something moving across his face. His first thought was *spider's web*, then he realised it was a pull string for the lights.

He pulled it. Suddenly, the whole stairwell lit up. He could see to the bottom of the staircase, but no further. "I've come this far," he said out loud, "may as well go the whole hog." He slowly made his way down the stairwell towards the darkness.

He was half way down when a voice said, "Not you again."

It was Simonds. "That's no place for you, Inspector. I would suggest you come back up."

Findlay looked at Simonds, then looked into the darkness at the bottom of the stairs. "Maybe you're right," he said and made his way back to the top.

Simonds closed the door behind them and locked it. He looked at Findlay and said, "Follow me."

Findlay followed him to the kitchen.

"Sit."

Findlay sat down at the kitchen table. Simonds sat opposite him.

"You don't have the map."

"I beg your pardon?" said Findlay.

"The map to the maze."

"What maze would that be?" said Findlay. "What on earth are you talking about?"

"The tunnels that run under the Manor," he said. "Miles of them. They were built hundreds of years ago by the monks when this place was a Priory. They built them as a maze to protect themselves during the reformation. They run for over two miles up to the old church on Chapel Hill. If you don't have the maze map, you will never be seen again. It's a rabbit warren under here. The map has been handed down through the generations. Only the Lord of the Manor has ever seen it, until Hannah Winton found it. She was only using his lordship as a cheque book, a meal ticket. She was having an affair with Robert. I think he convinced her to get the plan for him. He is after the Preston treasure; he actually believes it exists the fool.

"She told me she wanted to leave here with him, but she said he just laughed at her. He was using her, and she fell for his lies. She threatened to tell his lordship that he had copied the maze map, but she didn't get the chance to tell him, did she?"

"Are you telling me Robert Preston had a hand in the death of Hannah Winton?"

"No, I am not, Inspector. I'm simply telling you he had a good reason to see the back of her and Lord Preston. If his lordship had known what he was doing, he would have thrown him out, and I expect cut him off."

Findlay sat stunned. Like a light being switched on, every-thing was suddenly beginning to make sense.

Then he remembered Todd, Mardie, and Lady Victoria. They were heading for the tunnels.

"Oh, my word," said Findlay, "my sergeant is going down there!"

"Then I suggest you stop him, and quickly," said Simonds. "If they get too deep in, they may never come out again."

Findlay hurried from the Manor and ran across the court-yard towards the Annex.

"Sergeant Todd!" he shouted. But he was too late. It was then he realised he didn't even know where the entrance to the tunnels were.

He quickly returned to the main house and ran towards the kitchen. "Simonds!" he shouted.

Simonds appeared in the hallway.

"I was too late," said Findlay. "They are gone."

"Then there's nothing you can do, Inspector, except hope they mark the route they take."

CHAPTER 16

Todd held his torch in his outstretched hand. His other hand pressed against the tunnel walls as he tried to look into the darkness. Lady Victoria was behind him, followed by Mardie.

"It's so quiet down here," said Victoria.

"Yes, and cold," said Todd.

They reached a turning, which made Todd stop dead in his tracks. He pointed his torch ahead of him to show five tunnels.

"Oh, my god!" said Todd. He stood and stared for a few seconds. Then he said, "Which one?"

Mardie stepped forward. "This way," she said, and walked into the blackness of one of the tunnels. Todd and Victoria followed her.

"I think we should be leaving a mark," said Todd. "I wouldn't want to get lost down here."

"Well, it looks to me," said Victoria, "that she knows exactly where she is going."

They walked for what seemed an age until suddenly they found themselves standing in a cavern. Todd shone his torch around the walls. "Five more tunnels," he said. "This is amazing! Who built this? I have to admit, the deeper we go, the more nervous I'm getting."

"It's this way," said Mardie as once again she walked into one of the black entrances to a tunnel.

"This way," said Todd, pointing to the opening.

"No Sergeant, after you," said Victoria with a smile.

They were half walking, half stumbling down the tunnel for a few minutes when Victoria said, "Mardie seems to be very comfortable down here. I'm wondering how many times she has wandered through these tunnels."

"I was thinking the very same," said Todd.

Just then, Mardie stopped and pointed to the ceiling of the cave. "There be a ledge up there," she said. "That's where I found all my shiny things."

Todd shone his torch at the cave ceiling. "I think I can just about make that," he said.

"Be careful," said Victoria.

Todd backed up a few paces and ran at the wall. With one jump, he was clinging onto the ledge. He began pulling himself up slowly, he was getting closer. Then Mardie and Victoria grabbed a foot each and pushed. Todd pulled himself the last couple of feet, then rolled over and sat on the edge.

"Well done, Sergeant," said Victoria.

Todd just smiled and leaned over onto his side. "Ouch," he said.

"What's wrong?" shouted Victoria.

Todd didn't answer. He put his hand under his thigh and pulled from the dirt a solid gold crucifix about a foot in length. He sat mesmerised as it glinted in the light of his torch. He couldn't help thinking how heavy it was. He looked down and brushed away the dirt covering the rocks and ledge floor. There, laying in front of him, were three, four, no, six solid gold plates.

"Oh my," he exclaimed. He leaned over the edge. Mardie and Victoria stood, silently looking up at him. He held up the cross and one of the plates. "There's a fortune up here. It's everywhere," he said excitedly. "Every time I clear away dirt, there's more of it. It's a king's ransom just laying around. I need to look further in," he said. He turned onto his stomach and began crawling through the mass of dirt, dust and golden artefacts.

Findlay was nervously pacing up and down in the Manor hallway. Simonds appeared.

"Here," he said, holding out a piece of paper.

"What's this?" said Findlay.

"It's his Lordship's, or at least it was. It's the plan to the tunnels, you can get to them from here," he said, unlocking the cellar door. "And here's a torch."

Findlay stood at the top of the stairs. "I just know I'm going to regret this," he said out loud, but the thought of Todd being lost underground spurred him on. He made his way down the staircase. At the bottom, he switched on his torch.

He walked slowly down the tunnel. *I would know that smell anywhere,* he thought, *rats.*

He kept walking. Suddenly, he came to an old wooden ladder sticking out of a black hole. He shone his torch into the depths of the hole. *Oh well,* he thought, *here goes nothing,* and began climbing down.

The ladder seemed endless. He looked up. The entry hole to this hell seemed to have shrunk to half its size. Down and down, he went until at last he was on solid ground. Findlay turned around to see five tunnels in front of him.

The map, he thought, and pulled out the paper Simonds had given him. He shone his torch onto it. "Oh no," he said. "The map shows only four tunnels, and here we have five."

"The one on the left isn't on the map, so is that the one I follow? Why would it not be on the map? He stood and stared at it. He decided to take the fifth tunnel.

He cautiously made his way down the narrow tunnel, praying he had guessed right. He hadn't gone far when he heard voices, but they seemed to be coming from behind him. "But that's not possible, I just came from there." He was trying to make out what they were saying, but they were too far away, and echoing around the tunnel walls. He decided to keep going.

"Those voices," he said, "are they behind me, above me, or am I imagining them?" He kept walking until he reached a dead end. "Oh no," said Findlay, "no, no, not after coming this far." He shone his torch around the tunnel. No other way out. He was about to turn around and go back when he noticed scratches and gouges at the bottom of the wall. Findlay went down on one knee for a closer look.

He took a pen from his inside pocket and pushed it into the wall. The pen went in like a hot knife through butter. He stood up and, with one kick, the wall collapsed before him. Findlay found himself in a large cavern, still he could hear voices.

"Hello?" he shouted. His call echoed around the walls and tunnels.

"Hello?" he shouted again, "Sergeant Todd? Is that you?"

He stood very still and waited for the echoes to die away.

"Sir? Is that you?" came the reply.

"Yes!" he shouted. "Where are you, Sergeant?"

"I am up here, sir."

Findlay shone his torch at the roof of the cavern. There in the top corner was Todd, smiling down at him.

"Sergeant Todd," he said. "I've never been more pleased to see you. How do I get up there?"

"Stay where you are sir, I'll come down to you."

Findlay sat down on a rock, he shone his torch around the walls and ceiling of the cavern. He couldn't help but admire the monks of old. *They built this with nothing but the crudest of tools,* he thought. *I wonder how many died in its construction and how long it took them, all to save the riches of the church.*

It was then he heard footsteps. He stood up and saw Lady Victoria and Mardie walking towards him. At the back of them, carrying something over his shoulder, was Sergeant Todd.

"I'm so pleased to see you all," said Findlay. "For a while there, I was expecting to bump into Anubis."

Todd dropped his heavy burden on the ground. "Who sir?" said Todd.

"Anubis, the protector of tombs."

Todd shook his head.

"Never mind," said Findlay. "What on earth have you got there, Sergeant?"

"You're not going to believe this, sir!" Todd dropped his burden to the ground and opened up the jacket. Out fell a treasure trove of gold and silver artefacts encrusted with precious jewels.

Findlay stood and stared. "For once, Sergeant, you leave me dumbfounded."

"This isn't all of it," said Victoria.

"No sir, it's all I could carry."

"So, the Preston treasure really does exist," said Findlay.

"If only Lord Preston had made the effort," said Victoria. "Maybe he would still be alive."

Findlay walked over to Mardie. "You do realise all this belongs to the Church, although the finder's fee will be massive."

She nodded. "I know."

Findlay looked at her. *There's more going on behind those eyes than you think,* he thought to himself. Mardie raised an eyebrow and smiled.

"Come along, Sergeant, let me help you with this."

They gathered it all together and wrapped it in Todd's jacket.

"I think it will be easier to go back this way than drag it back up there."

They made the long trip back to the ladder. "Up you go Sergeant, I'm not about to try and pull that up there, not with my back."

Todd slowly pulled the heavy weight up the ladder. At the top, he pulled it through the hole and collapsed panting on the kitchen floor. Mardie, Victoria, then Findlay pulled themselves out and into the daylight.

"Now what, sir?" asked Todd.

"First thing is to report the find to the coroner. That's the law I'm afraid."

Todd looked dejected. "I was getting used to being very wealthy," he quipped.

At that, the kitchen door opened. It was Robert and Edward.

"Simonds said you were down here, and what do we have here?" said Robert.

"Oh my god," said Edward, "you've found it, you've actually found it!"

"If you mean we have found the treasure belonging to the Catholic Church, then yes," said Findlay, "we have found it. It must now be handed over to the appropriate authorities to be assessed."

"What!" shouted Robert. "You can't be serious."

"I'm very serious," said Findlay. "It's classed as treasure trove and belongs to the crown. It will be assessed and eventually handed back to the Church. That is the law."

"Should I go back for the rest, sir?" said Todd.

"There's more?" exclaimed Robert and Edward almost in unison.

Findlay gave Todd that look. "Well done, Sergeant."

"Yes," he said, "a lot more, from all accounts. I will need to get to a phone and get help up here."

Robert kicked the kitchen door, and it slammed shut. "You're not going anywhere," said Robert, pulling a revolver from his jacket pocket. "Over there," he motioned to Victoria and Mardie. "And you," he said to Todd.

"Don't be ridiculous," said Findlay. "What are you going to do, shoot all four of us?"

Robert said nothing. He waved the revolver around while pointing it at Mardie. "If I have to," he said.

"And what about you Edward? Is this what you want?"

"No," he said. "No, it isn't what I want. Put the gun down, brother."

"They are trying to steal our inheritance," shouted Robert.

"Like the Inspector said, what are you going to do? It doesn't belong to us, it never has."

"Well, I'm not giving it up that easily," shouted Robert.

CHAPTER 17

Suddenly, Edward grabbed Robert's arm and went for the revolver. The two brothers struggled for control, then fell onto the kitchen floor. Two loud bangs rang out, which echoed around the whole Manor. The two brothers lay on the floor, staring at each other.

"Robert," said Edward, "what have you made me do?"

Edward rose to his feet, holding the gun which he threw onto the kitchen table.

Victoria and Mardie were cowering in the corner when Findlay said, "Sergeant, take a look."

Todd went down on his knees and checked, he looked at Findlay and shook his head.

"Oh my god," said Edward. "I've killed him, my brother, I've killed him!"

Suddenly, Mardie stepped forward and stood over the lifeless body of Robert Preston. She was smiling.

Findlay stood next to her with a very confused look on his face. "Mardie," he said, "are you alright?"

"I am now, Inspector," she said. "That's both of them gone."

"I don't understand Mardie, what are you saying?"

"I have waited a long time for this day," she said. "I was just a little girl when my father went looking for Lord Preston after a night of drinking. He couldn't live with the knowledge that he and my mother had an affair, and as you now know,

I was the result of that love triangle. My father tried to kill him, but he failed. Robert saw everything. He decided to do something about it, so ordered Simonds to do something to my father's car. I don't know if he did or not, but I think he did. I can't prove that, but that's what I believe. My mother had a doctor's appointment on that fateful morning, so I was left in the care of Robert and Edward's nanny. My mother and father were both in the car when the brakes failed. They both died that day. Lord Preston and Robert got what they deserved. Preston may have been my biological father, but Jack Ellis was my real father. Never Preston, he never was."

"How do you know all this?" asked Victoria.

"Robert took great pleasure in tormenting me. He would go out of his way to remind me that if it wasn't for his nanny, I would be dead. You have no idea how much I hated that pig. I've lived in squalor, gone hungry, and have taken his abuse for years. Now it's all over. The only drawback with the poison that killed Lord Preston was that it was too quick."

"So, you know about poisons, Mardie?"

She smiled. "Of course I do, Inspector. I'm a gardener. It's my job to know."

"What about Hannah Winton?" asked Todd.

"She shouldn't have taken the car," said Mardie. "She was an accident."

"Are you admitting to murdering Lord Preston and Hannah Winton?" asked Findlay.

"Don't be ridiculous, Inspector, I'm just a lowly gardener. Of course, you will never prove any of this. The finger of guilt points squarely at Robert Preston. After all, he is the one who stood to gain by his father's death, not me. I'm just a fool of a gardener, until Lady Victoria found that file, of course, and I became the Lady of Chelston Manor."

"So, it was you who broke the seal," said Victoria. "You've known all along that Lord Preston was your father, and that you would inherit the estate."

Mardie just smiled. "Unfortunately for you, Inspector, your only suspect is now dead, dead from a gunshot, not poison, and he was a chemist, well versed in poisons. It's obvious to me that he killed Hannah and his father." She smiled again and walked out of the kitchen.

Findlay, Todd, and Victoria stood in silence. "Well, well, never judge a book by its cover," said Todd.

"I must get to a phone," said Findlay.

"What about me?" asked Edward.

"I think you are as much a victim here as your father and Hannah Winton were. For now, I must have this area cleared, and Sergeant, don't let anyone in. Oh, and leave that treasure trove where it is for now."

"What about my brother?" asked Edward.

"It was self-defence. An accident even, you won't be held responsible. Mardie, or should I say Maria, had us all fooled. She can't be allowed to get away with this," said Findlay. "I'm still not convinced by her story though."

CHAPTER 18

That night, he was sitting at his kitchen table, filling out his official report on the day's events. Mrs Findlay sat down opposite him. "Drink your tea dear, it's getting cold."

"I will," he replied. "I just need to get all of this down on paper. Nobody is going to believe it. I actually think Mardie will get away with this," he said. "I can't prove any of it. She is right. Everything points to Robert Preston."

"So, you're saying the only one who could prove Mardie is the killer is now dead?"

"Yes dear," said Findlay.

"So, you think if the brothers hadn't fought and Robert hadn't been shot, then Mardie would have killed him?"

"In my opinion, dear, sooner or later, yes."

"What if he was still alive? Would she go after him?"

"Yes, probably. He's the only one standing between her and the Preston millions, and she blames him above all for the death of her parents."

Findlay stared at her. "Okay, I have known you long enough to know when you're cooking something up."

"Just give me a moment dear, let me think, just for a moment." She stood up and walked over to the sink, picked up a plate, and started drying it.

Findlay said nothing, he just sat and watched her.

Suddenly she said, "Let her believe he's still alive, that he's in the hospital. Tell her it's touch and go, it's not looking good, but there's a chance he might pull through. That should be enough to force her to try and finish him. Put Sergeant Todd in the hospital bed. She won't know with the curtains closed. When she strikes, you will have her."

"Good Lord," said Findlay, "sometimes you frighten me. How would you even think of something like that?"

"It's a woman thing, dear."

Findlay smiled. "I must remember never to upset you," he said.

The next morning, Findlay was sitting having his morning pot of tea and toast.

"Good morning dear," said Mrs Findlay. "You didn't sleep very well, did you? I heard you pacing up and down."

"Good morning," he replied. "No, I didn't. I couldn't get what you said out of my mind. I think it could actually work. I'll speak to Todd, see what he thinks."

"That's right, dear," she said. "I knew you would figure it out."

Findlay smiled. "Yes dear, of course."

He picked up his trilby hat, gloves and coat, kissed Mrs Findlay on the cheek and said, "Bye bye, my love, see you later." And left for the office.

Todd met Sally in the old school shop cafe in the village. He was already there when Sally arrived.

"Hi," she said.

"Morning Sal. Pot of tea?"

"Yes please," she said.

Todd ordered tea for two and sat next to Sally. She reached out and took his hand. "I hear you had quite a day of it yesterday?"

Todd shook his head. "You don't know the half of it," he said.

He told her the story and about the fortune he found in the tunnels. Sally sat and listened, stunned by what he was telling her.

"Oh," she said, "how awful. While I was standing behind the bar in the Drum chatting, you were going through all that."

"It's my job, Sal. That's what I do. Anyway," he said, "I wasn't alone. Lady Victoria was with me."

"Really?" she said.

"Yes, Mardie had her fooled as well."

He could see she wasn't very happy. "Sal, what's wrong?"

"Nothing," she said.

Todd looked at his watch. "Oh no, I'm late. I'll have to go. Will I see you later?"

"Yes, of course," she said.

Todd put a two-shilling coin on the table. He bent down and gave her a kiss. "I'll see you later."

He soon reached his office fully expecting the Inspector to read him the riot act for being late.

"Good morning, Sergeant."

"Morning, sir," he said tentatively.

Todd slowly sat at his desk. He was waiting for it, but nothing came. "Everything alright, sir?"

"Yes, Sergeant, everything is fine. The coroner cleaned up the mess at the Manor. The treasure trove is now in their possession, or at least what you managed to carry out. The remains of Robert Preston are at the Torquay mortuary. A straightforward case, I think. Another treasure trip will be called for, otherwise yes, everything is fine."

Todd just stared at him. "Okay," he said. "Good."

"How are things going with Sally and yourself?"

"Really good, sir, thank you."

"That's nice," said Findlay.

"Yes sir," said Todd. He had known Findlay long enough to know when something was coming. It was just a case of what, and when, he thought.

"Cuppa?" said Findlay.

"Right," said Todd, "what's going on? I've been here nearly eight years and not once have you offered me a cup of tea. Plus, I was late again this morning, third time this week, and the roof is still on."

"Yes," said Findlay. "I did notice."

"So, what's going on, sir? Put me out of my misery. I just know I'm not going to like it, whatever it is."

"You have such a suspicious nature," said Findlay, pouring two cups of tea. "Remind me, Sergeant, sugar?"

"Yes sir, two please."

Findlay picked up his cup of tea and took it to his desk.

CHAPTER 19

"Well?" said Todd. "Let's have it."

"There is something," said Findlay. "We both know Mardie is mixed up in this, not Robert Preston. Proving it will be virtually impossible. It turns out that poor downtrodden girl was quicker and brighter than all of us. The only way she will be brought to justice is if we could catch her with the Wolfsbane poison."

"That's never going to happen now, sir, or is it?"

"Funny you should say that, Sergeant. There may well be a way of catching her red handed, but it will mean some personal risk."

Todd listened intently, then he said, "I take it that personal risk, is mine?"

"Correct," said Findlay. "You're about the right build and height to pull this off. I want you to go into Torbay hospital. You will be in a private ward, a side room. You will be wired up to machines, or at least it will look that way. A rumour that Robert Preston is still alive will be circulated around the village. When Mardie finds out he's still alive, she will, I hope, come for him. While Robert Preston is alive, she will never inherit the estate. If this goes well, Edward Preston will become the new Lord of the Manor."

Todd sat and looked at him. "So, you want me to pretend to be Robert Preston so she can poison me? You want me to lay in a hospital bed while a psychotic gardener tries to kill me, and you want me to do this because you made me a cup of tea?"

"Well," said Findlay, "when you put it like that, it does sound mercenary, but yes, you're right."

Todd shook his head. "Fine, if that's what it will take, then I will do it."

"Just one thing, Sergeant. Nobody can know about this, absolutely nobody."

"But sir, how will I explain my disappearing for days to Sally?"

"I said nobody, Sergeant."

"Yes sir, understood."

"Now," said Findlay, "I need to go to Torbay hospital and make some arrangements. You hold the fort here. I won't be long." Findlay collected his coat and left.

Todd sat mulling over what had been said while sipping his tea. Suddenly, Inspector Findlay's phone started to ring. Todd picked it up. "Good morning, Cockington police."

"Oh," said a voice, "Is that you Allan?"

"It is," he replied.

"It's Mrs Findlay, is my husband there?"

"I'm afraid not. You just missed him, but he shouldn't be long. Is everything alright? You sound a little shaken."

"I take it you haven't been listening to the radio?" she asked.

"No, we haven't. Why?"

"The news has just been on. Mr Chamberlain just gave a speech. The worst thing has happened. Germany has invaded Poland," she said. "The man on the radio said we could be at war with Germany by the end of the month."

"Good god!" said Todd. "No, I hadn't heard. As soon as the Inspector returns, I will get him to phone you."

At that, Mrs Findlay just hung up.

Todd replaced the phone and sat back in his chair. "Well, I never," he said.

He won't even be at the hospital yet, he thought. *No point just sitting here, I'll pop down the Drum and see Sally.*

It took just a few minutes for him to reach the Drum. He pushed open the pub door. Sally was standing behind the bar.

"Allan," she said, "what a surprise. Have you heard the news?"

"If you mean about Germany invading Poland, yes. Mrs F just rang the office. To be honest, she sounded quite upset, not like her."

"Where's the Inspector?" asked Sally.

"Oh, he..." he stopped himself just in time. "He's on business," he said. "Police business. He will be back soon, so I can't stay long. I just wanted to see you."

"How lovely," said Sally. "You missed me then?" she said with a huge smile.

"Yes, actually I did. I heard the news about a possible war heading our way, and I just felt I had to see you."

There were two men standing quietly at the bar, drinking their beer. They both looked at him and grinned. "I thinks you got it bad, boy," said one of them. "Think I'll be out buying a new hat for the wedding soon," said the other. They both started laughing.

Todd glared at them. "This is a private conversation, if you don't mind," he said.

The two men laughed and took their drinks to one of the alcove booths.

"We do need a chat, Sal," he said.

"Oh? Should I be worried?"

"No," said Todd, "not at all. It's just that I might have to go away for a few days. Police business."

Sally looked at him. "Police business?" she said.

"Training," said Todd, "just training. But I will be gone for a few days."

"I suppose I should get used to it," she said.

"I'm afraid so, my love, the joys of being with a copper. Anyway, I better get back. I was late again this morning. He wasn't happy."

Sally smiled. "I can't imagine why you would be late." And winked at him.

"Sally Donnelly. Really!" said Todd as he kissed her on the cheek. "I'll see you later."

"You'd better," she said, and he left.

He arrived back at his office just as Findlay climbed out of his car.

"Been somewhere, Sergeant?"

"Not far, sir, not far."

CHAPTER 20

The two men made their way up to the office and sat behind their desks.

"Right, Sergeant, it's organised. They are expecting you this afternoon."

"This afternoon?" said Todd. "That's quick."

"We don't have time to play games. If Robert Preston is supposed to be alive, it has to be today."

"I said I would see Sally later."

"You will have plenty of time for stepping out," said Findlay, "when this is all over. I've arranged for the news of Robert Preston's remarkable recovery to spread. Mrs Findlay will mention it at her flower arranging class this afternoon; that will do it. It will reach Mardie's ears very quickly. So, Sergeant, let's get you into your hospital bed."

"I feel bad, sir. Sally won't know where I am if I just vanish. I told her I was going on a training course."

"If she's going to become a copper's wife, she will have to get used to it. I will have a word with her," said Findlay. "I'll tell her your course was brought forward and you'll be back in a few days. It's a white lie Sergeant, you can explain to her later. Come along, let's get this done."

Mrs Findlay arrived at her monthly flower arranging class to find it full.

"My word," she said. "I have never seen so many members at one time."

"They are here for the gossip," said her instructor. "Word has got around about the Preston treasure and that Robert Preston was found with his throat slit from ear to ear."

"Who on earth told you that?" she protested.

"There was a struggle between him and his brother. Did his brother cut his throat?" asked one of the ladies.

"No," she said. "And his throat wasn't cut! They struggled and Robert Preston's revolver went off and shot him."

The whole class was now standing around her, desperate for the gossip.

"What about the treasure?" asked another. "How much is it worth?"

"I have no idea," said Mrs Findlay. "It's all in the hands of the coroner."

"We heard he was dead?"

"No, he isn't dead."

"What!" they said. "He's not dead?"

"He's in Torbay hospital as we speak. He's very, very poorly, but he should pull through."

At that, she carried on arranging her flowers.

"Well, I never," said one of the ladies. "Well, I never."

Mrs Findlay looked around her. The whole class was talking about it. "Well, my job's done," she thought to herself. "I just hope Allan is ready."

Todd was already in his hospital gown and tucked up in bed.

Findlay pulled the curtains across. "That should do it, Sergeant."

"What do I do, sir?"

"Nothing, just lay still, you've been shot, remember?"

"Can't I even read a paper?"

"No, you cannot. Now lay down and keep still. I will sit in the bathroom and watch."

"But sir, we don't even know that she's heard the news."

"Oh, I guarantee she has. You don't know the Cockington flower arranging circle!"

Sally had just finished her shift at the Drum.

"Night Sal," said Marjory the landlady.

"Night night," replied Sally. "See you tomorrow, god willing."

She slowly made her way up Cockington Lane towards the village centre. She checked her watch, nine-thirty. *I've just got enough time before going to Allan's,* she thought.

Findlay was sitting in the darkness of the bathroom, struggling to keep his eyes open. He peered through the crack in the door. Todd was lying on his side, snoring like an old bull.

"Sergeant," he muttered. "Sergeant Todd, will you wake up?" But Todd continued to snore.

Findlay shook his head and slowly pulled a paper bag from his pocket. He opened it up and pulled out a beef sandwich. "Mrs F thinks of everything," he mused and continued peering through the crack in the side of the door as he enjoyed what was in effect his evening meal.

Sally arrived at Mrs Bruce's house where Todd had lodgings and knocked on the door.

Mrs Bruce answered. "Sally," she said, "what a surprise."

"I'm here to meet Allan."

"I'm sorry dear, he's not here."

"That's strange," said Sally. "He arranged to meet me here. I'm actually a little bit early."

"Do come in. I expect he just got held up at work. I will put the kettle on."

Sally thanked her and Mrs Bruce showed her through to the best room. They sat and chatted for about an hour about this and that.

Eventually, Sally said she would just go home. "It's close to ten-thirty, too late to do anything. Could you tell him I'm not happy, please?"

"Yes dear, I will. He should have at least phoned; his dinner is in the oven."

Sally made her way home, oblivious to what was going on at the hospital.

Todd was fast asleep. It was warm, quiet, dark, and peaceful.

Findlay had fallen into a deep sleep. He sat with his arms folded, his head down in a world of his own. He was suddenly awakened by the sound of a phone ringing in the main ward. He raised his head and rubbed his eyes. He couldn't believe he had actually fallen asleep.

He peered through the side of the door. It was dark, he couldn't see much. He was about to sit back in his seat when he saw the outline of something or somebody. He leaned forward again and put his eye to the opening in the door. "Oh my god," he thought, "there's somebody in there with Todd."

He decided no point in waiting. He couldn't see anything anyway. It was too dark. He jumped up and threw open the bathroom door. "Stop!" he shouted. "Police!"

Sergeant Todd woke with a fright. Instinctively, he grabbed the arm of the intruder and fell out of his bed, dragging himself and whoever it was to the ground.

Findlay switched on the light, there laying in front of him, was Todd holding on tightly to the arm of a young nurse.

"What the hell are you doing?" she screamed.

"What are you doing in here?" shouted Findlay. "This is a police operation, you're not supposed to be here."

"I didn't know that," she said. "I've just come on duty, nobody told me."

"Right," said Findlay, "get up, Sergeant, and help that poor girl."

"Sorry," said Todd, "I'm so sorry."

"It's not your fault," she said. "What's your name?"

"Todd, Allan Todd."

"I'm Julie," she said.

"And I'm Inspector Findlay and I'm angry, tired, fed up, and worried. Now, if you don't mind?" He opened the ward door. "Thank you," he said. "If we need you, we will call you." And he closed the door behind her.

"It's after twelve, Sergeant. Let's get back to work. And Sergeant? Try to stay awake!"

Todd climbed back into his bed and Findlay took up his chair in the bathroom.

The hours ticked by, Findlay yawned and looked at his watch. "Three forty-five," he muttered. "I should be home in bed."

It was then he heard the handle on the ward door creaking as it turned. He sat very still and held his breath. He peered through the crack. It was Mardie. She stood silhouetted against the glass ward door. He looked at Todd, who he thought looked fast asleep. Findlay knew he had to wait. So far, she had done nothing wrong. He was sure she would hear his heart beating, so he pressed his hand against his chest to quieten it down. He sat motionless and watched.

After what seemed an age, she put a hand into her pocket and took something out. He couldn't see what it was. Every fibre of his body wanted to jump up, but he had to have the proof, so he waited.

She slowly walked over to the bed until she was just a few inches away. She bent over the still body in the bed when suddenly the lights from a car passing the window lit up the room. She realised it wasn't Robert Preston. She recognised Todd and stood bolt upright.

Todd wasn't asleep. He grabbed her arm and pulled her across the bed while swinging his body out and held her firmly down. She struggled to get free, but Todd wasn't about to let go.

Finlay flicked on the lights. "Well, Mardie, I knew you would have to come. And what's this?"

He leaned over the bed and picked up a syringe.

"That's nothing to do with me," she protested.

"I'm willing to bet that whatever is in here is the same thing that killed Hannah Winton and Lord Preston," said Findlay. "I was ready to arrest Robert Preston. I never gave a thought to you having that kind of knowledge, but it all makes sense now. If only your anger hadn't gotten the better of you, you would have had it all."

"Maria Diane Preston, I'm arresting you on suspicion of involvement in the deaths of Hannah Winton and Lord David Preston. You do not have to say anything, but anything you do say may be used against you in a court of law. Do you understand?"

Mardie did not reply.

"Sergeant, restrain her. Oh, and Sergeant? Please put some trousers on!"

Mardie was led by Findlay down the corridor and out to the police car.

"I actually felt sorry for you," he said. "My wife and I were even talking about taking you in."

He opened the car door. She climbed in the back and Findlay locked her in.

Todd made his way to the car park, still getting dressed as he walked.

"Allan?" said a voice. It was Julie, the ward nurse.

"Hi," said Todd. "It's Julie, isn't it?"

"Yes. I'm free after six tonight if you fancy going for a drink?"

Todd smiled and cleared his throat. "Thanks for the invitation," he said, "but I have somebody that I love very, very much."

"Lucky girl," said Julie. "Oh well, never mind. Another time maybe?"

Todd just smiled.

CHAPTER 21

Mardie was taken back to Cockington station, where she would be transferred that night to Plymouth.

"Sergeant," said Findlay, "Sally will be looking for you. At least we didn't have to lie to her about your training. Go on. I'll see you tomorrow."

"Tomorrow sir?"

"Yes," said Findlay, "you can have the rest of the day off. You've earned it."

"Thanks," he said.

Todd made his way home. He looked at his watch. It was seven-thirty in the morning. The thought of his own comfortable bed made him smile. He quietly opened the front door, removed his shoes, and crept in. He slowly made his way to the stairs when suddenly the hallway light went on.

"And what time do you call this?" said Mrs Bruce.

"Mrs Bruce," he said with a start. "Don't you know you could give a man a heart attack doing that?"

"I'll heart attack you," she said. "Sally sat and waited until ten-thirty or more. I'll tell you this, she was not happy with you. You've got some explaining to do. And your dinner was ruined."

"Oh," he said, "sorry, is it in the oven?"

"No," she replied, "it's in next door's dog. You'll have to wait for breakfast."

"I'm fine," said Todd. "I'm just so tired, I've been up all night. I think I'll just go up to bed. I will see Sally later and explain."

"Why were you up all night?" asked Mrs Bruce.

"It's too long a story, would you mind if I told you about it later, please?"

"If you must," she said. "If Sally calls, what do I tell her?"

Todd raised his eyebrows. "I've no idea," he said. "Just tell her I'm fine and I'll see her later and explain everything." At that, he made his way up the stairs to his room.

Findlay arrived home to a welcome from Mrs Findlay. "How did it go, darling?"

"Exactly as we thought it would," he said. "I've never been so bored. Todd was snoring like an old bull while I sat on a wooden chair hiding in the bathroom. I must admit, I didn't expect her to show up so quickly, but she did. She's been arrested, and I'm waiting for transport to arrive from Plymouth."

He stood and stared out of the window.

"Go on," said Mrs Findlay, "something is bothering you. What is it?"

"I don't know," said Findlay. "It was too easy; it was all just too easy. She must have known we would be watching her. That there would be a guard on his room, and she still came, armed with the evidence. It doesn't feel right."

He started putting his coat on.

"What are you doing?" she asked.

"It's no good," said Findlay. "It just doesn't feel right. I need to talk to her before they take her to Plymouth. I'll be back as soon as I can."

Mrs Findlay held open the front door. "Nothing I can say will stop you, I don't suppose?"

"No, dear."

"Very well, don't be long."

Findlay smiled, kissed her on the cheek, and walked over to his car.

Todd sat on the end of his bed. He had tried to sleep, but Mrs Bruce's words were going around in his head. "That's it," he said, and began getting dressed. "I'm not going to get a wink of sleep until I've seen Sally."

He pulled on his coat and made his way down towards the street.

Mrs Bruce stood in the hallway. "You'll have plenty of time to sleep later, Allan," she said.

He smiled as he closed the door behind him.

He quickly made his way down to the Drum where Sally lived. He put two fingers in his mouth and blew hard. A high-pitched whistle echoed around the empty car park and adjoining fields.

Sally appeared at the top window, still in her dressing gown. "She doesn't look happy," he muttered. He put on his best smile and she pointed to the side door.

Todd stood with his hands in his pockets with his breath steaming into the morning air. The side door opened. "This better be good," said Sally.

"If you let me in, I'll explain everything."

Sally turned and walked into the bar area, with Todd following. "Well?" she said. "Let's hear it."

Todd explained the whole evening to her. Right down to being the bait in the trap. It was at that point that Sally exploded. "You actually lay in a bed and waited for some deranged female to come and kill you? You actually did that?!"

It was then that he realised maybe he had given away too much information.

"I was quite safe. The Inspector was watching everything, and Julie was just outside the door in case we needed her."

Sally went quiet. "Who's Julie? And why, if you are in bed, is she just outside of the door?"

"No," said Todd. "I didn't mean it to come out that way. She's a nurse at Torbay. Had we needed medical care, she was on hand."

Todd put his arms around her. "Come on Sal, you know I wouldn't do anything to upset you, it's just my job. It's no different to you being behind the bar. You're pleasant and chat and smile at everyone, because it's your job. Being a copper and dealing with the things that entails is mine. I love you Sal, you have to trust me. If it's like this now, what's it going to be like if we got married?"

"Married?" gasped Sally. "Allan Todd, have you just proposed to me?"

"Well... well yes. Kind of... yes. I mean, yes, I think I did."

"Then my answer is yes!" screamed Sally. She threw her arms around him and passionately kissed him.

"Oh Allan. Wait until I tell mum and dad. You've made me so very happy. You did mean it, didn't you? I mean, you won't change your mind?"

Allan smiled and looked her in the eye. "Why?" he said. "Why would I change my mind? I love you. I want to spend the rest of my days with you."

She kissed him again, then jumped up. "Right," she said, "you go and get some sleep. I must get dressed. I've got so many people to tell, this is so exciting. Oh, and Allan? I have not yet fully forgiven you for putting yourself at risk, but we will save that conversation for another day. Go," she said, shooing him out of the door. "Go and sleep."

He slowly walked out, wide eyed and wondering what just happened. *Oh my,* he thought, *I just asked Sally to marry me. Or did I? Yes, I did. I think.*

His mind was racing as he arrived back at Mrs Bruce's lodging house. As he walked through the door, she shouted, "Allan, is that you?"

"Yes, it's me."

"Did you explain yourself to Sally?"

"I did," he said quietly.

Mrs Bruce came down the stairs. "I asked if you explained yourself to Sally," she said.

"She did. I mean, I did," he said. "I think?"

"You really do need some sleep. I've turned down your bed and put you a hot water bottle in. Go on, up you go."

Todd just nodded and slowly made his way to his room.

CHAPTER 22

Findlay had arrived at Cockington police station. He was sitting quietly in a small office that doubled as the interview room, mulling over everything that had happened.

The desk sergeant came in. "If you're ready, Inspector? We can bring her through."

Findlay nodded. He decided he would get nowhere if he waited for her to tell the truth. The office door opened, and she was shown in. "Hello Mardie," he said, "please sit down."

She just stood.

"Please yourself," said Findlay. "Why are you doing this, Mardie?"

She just stared at him.

"I know you didn't kill Lord Preston or Hannah Winton. It just doesn't make any sense. You're angry, yes, but you're no killer. I also know that you're not the quiet, little, backward gardener you make yourself out to be. So, who are you protecting?"

She said nothing. She just stood and stared at him.

Findlay stood up. "Is it Simonds? Is he the guilty one? Or maybe it's Edward Preston?" he said.

"I'm trying to help you Mardie. If you're found guilty, you will go to prison for the rest of your life. That's if you're lucky. You could go to the gallows. So who is worth taking that risk for, and why?"

He stood quietly to see her reaction, but there was none.

"Your life has been one of pain and sorrow, I understand that, but don't throw the rest of it away. Talk to me, tell me what's been going on. Let me help you."

She still said nothing.

"Very well. If you change your mind, I will come to Plymouth to see you."

"Plymouth?" she said.

Findlay was amazed she had actually spoken. "Yes," he said. "They are taking you to Plymouth. You'll be held there until more evidence is collected, then a court date will be set. It could be months away. Mardie? You're shaking."

"Don't let them send me to Plymouth. I want to stay here, in Cockington."

"That's not possible," said Findlay. "Do you understand what is happening? Why you are here, what you're being accused of?"

"I've done nothing wrong, sir," she said. "I haven't done nothing."

"But Mardie, you came to Torbay hospital looking for Robert Preston. You brought a needle; you were going to kill him."

"I was not. I was told to bring it."

"Who told you Mardie? Who gave you the needle and told you to bring it to that hospital room?"

She didn't answer him.

"Mardie, for god's sake, speak to me! Otherwise, I can't help you."

"I can't," she said. "I just can't."

Findlay was shocked. He was suddenly seeing her as she was. For the first time in his long career, he didn't know where to go. He knew she was innocent, but for some inexplicable reason, she wouldn't give up her secret.

"I have to leave you," he said.

"Please don't leave me," she pleaded.

"I'm sorry," he said, "I have to."

Findlay left the room. His intuition was proven right, but what to do now.

He left Cockington police station and walked slowly through the village. In the centre, opposite the forge, was an old wooden bench he and Mrs Findlay spent many happy hours sitting on and watching the world go by, and the many horse riders that visited the forge. He sat down and laid his top coat over his knee. He took off his hat and raised his face up to the sun.

"What to do?" he muttered. "What do I do?" He sat motionless for a few seconds,

"Lady Victoria," he said out loud. "Of course. If anyone can get through to Mardie, it will be her."

CHAPTER 23

H e quickly made his way back to his car, jumped in, and made his way to Chelston Manor. He was amazed to see as he pulled into the driveway, Beth the coroner, and several vans with men in white jackets. He climbed out of his car and stood watching them running in and out of the Manor.

"Beth!" he shouted. "What's all this? What's going on?"

"The Preston treasure," she said. "There's a lot more of it than we thought. Archaeologists from all over the country are pouring in looking for a chance to search. It's already being called the Cockington Hoard. It's worth millions," she said quietly, "absolute millions. Whoever ends up getting the finder's fee will be very, very wealthy. Anyway, what are you doing here? You haven't found another body for me, have you?"

"No Beth, I haven't. I'm here for a chat with Lady Victoria."

"By the way," she said, "the syringe you gave me? Saline."

"What?" said Findlay.

"Saline water and sugar," she said. "I'm afraid it's more fattening than deadly."

Findlay stood and stared. "Water and sugar?"

"Yes," she said, "harmless saline."

Beth went to join her colleagues in the Manor while Findlay sat down on the marble steps.

"Why would somebody give her a perfectly harmless syringe and send her into the hospital?"

"Inspector, good morning."

It was Lady Victoria.

Findlay stood up. "Hello," he said. "I was on my way to see you."

Findlay told her about Mardie and the syringe.

"Why?" said Victoria. "What could possibly be gained from setting that poor girl up?"

"I have no idea," said Findlay. "She's being taken to Plymouth tomorrow. She's terrified, but she still won't talk to me. Somebody has her so frightened that she is prepared to go to prison rather than give them up. I need someone to talk to her, someone she trusts. She has to tell somebody what's going on."

"You want me to talk to her?"

"Yes, I do," said Findlay. "Either Edward Preston or Simonds are involved somewhere along the line. I need to know what she knows or I can't help her."

"Of course, Inspector, I can come now if it suits?"

"It does," he replied.

They made their way to Cockington. On the way Victoria asked, "So she's said nothing, no names, no reason, nothing?"

"No," said Findlay, "not a word."

They reached Cockington station. Findlay held the station door open and Lady Victoria entered.

Findlay called the desk sergeant over, "Lady Victoria will be having a word with the prisoner. She can use my office; see they are not disturbed."

Findlay pulled out the chair, and she sat down. "They will bring her through in a moment. I'll be in the next room. See if you can get anything out of her."

"I'll try," she said, "but I still don't see why she would talk to me. But I will try for you."

Finlay smiled and closed the office door.

Victoria heard footsteps echoing along the corridor and muffled voices. The door opened and there stood Mardie.

"Just bang on the door when you want to leave," said the sergeant. He closed the door and turned the key with a click.

Victoria stood up. "Mardie," she said, "come sit down please."

Mardie walked slowly over and sat down.

"Well, well, well," said Victoria, "what a mess this is, isn't it?"

Mardie nodded.

"The inspector said you won't speak to him, or give him any names, is that right?"

Mardie kept her head bowed and nodded.

"Have you spoken to anyone else about this?" she asked.

Mardie slowly shook her head. "No," she said.

"It'd better stay that way," said Lady Victoria. "You know what will happen if you talk, don't you? Eventually, I will inherit everything. There's just Edward to take care of now. If you speak one word, I promise you, I will do what I said I would do. I will have every tree, every bush, every flower ripped from the ground at Chelston Manor. Especially the remembrance garden for your parents that you are so proud of. I will make sure nothing ever grows at Chelston Manor ever again. As for that wooden box you live in, that you call home, that will be the first thing to go. Do you understand?"

Mardie, with her head still bowed, nodded.

"Good. As long as you continue taking the blame, everything will be fine," she said with a smile. "They can't prove anything. It still looks like Robert killed his father and Hannah Winton, then was accidentally shot in a struggle with his brother. As soon as Edward is out of the way, everything will be fine. As for the syringe, it contained only water and sugar. They can't even prove you brought it in. So, keep denying everything. Do you understand?"

Mardie looked up, tears in her eyes. She would rather go to prison than see her and her late father's work destroyed. Again, she nodded. "Please," she said, "please don't kill all my beautiful trees and woodlands. I'll do what you ask."

Lady Victoria stood up and walked over to the door. She put her hand on Mardie's shoulder as she passed. "Good girl," she said with a smile.

She was about to bang on the door when it opened. Standing in front of her was Inspector Findlay, Sergeant Todd, and two female police officers. She took a step back. "Inspector," she said, "what's going on?"

"I knew something wasn't right. It was all too easy. It was the syringe that caught you," he said. "I know you think we couldn't prove anything, but I had the coroner do some checking. Lord Preston suffered with diabetes, he had to inject daily. She checked with the pharmacy. The syringe he used was special. It had a thicker plunger. Lord Preston had arthritis in his hands. The thicker plunger made it easier for him to push. Only one company makes them. That's Tyler's in Bristol, and Lord Preston is their only customer in this part of Devon."

"You will never prove any of this," said Victoria.

"We don't have to," said Findlay. "Ever heard of an intercom system? It's a new thing. What's it called again, Sergeant?"

"Technology, sir."

"Yes, that's it, new technology. We were standing in the outside office and listened to you admitting to everything. It also automatically records on reel-to-reel tape. So, my Lady, gotcha!"

"Lady Victoria Preston, I am arresting you for the murder of Lord David Preston and Hannah Winton. You do not have to say anything, but anything you do say will be taken down and could be used against you in a court of law. Sergeant Todd, do the honours."

"My pleasure, sir."

Sergeant Todd clipped his handcuffs around Victoria's wrists. "To think I actually liked you," he whispered.

She looked him in the eye and smiled. "No accounting for taste, Sergeant."

The two police officers took her away.

Mardie just sat and watched. "Am I still in trouble, sir?"

"No Mardie, you are not."

Sergeant Todd removed her handcuffs.

"I still have a few things I need to ask you," he said. "But for now, I think a hot drink is called for."

"I'll get it, sir," said Todd.

"No, thank you, Sergeant, this young lady has had enough trouble without being made to drink your tea."

The three of them sat down.

"We know why you did what you did, but I have to ask you, did you give Lady Preston the poison?"

"No sir, I did not. My dad, he taught me when I was little to never touch that stuff. I always burn it and kills it when I sees it."

"So, Inspector," said Todd, "it looks like Robert Preston gave the poison to Victoria to get rid of his father. Unfortunately, Hannah Winton got caught in the middle."

"It looks that way, yes. Oh, what a tangled web we weave..."

"Sorry sir?"

"Nothing, Sergeant, nothing. Now you, young lady, are coming home with me. Mrs Findlay has a bed made up for you and if I know her, a bottle warming the sheets as we speak. Tomorrow, Mardie, we will sort out your future for you. God knows you've earned it."

Findlay stood up. "I'll see you in the morning, Sergeant."

"Yes sir," said Todd. "I do need to talk to you about Sally, and I..."

"Yes, yes, Sergeant, tomorrow."

CHAPTER 24

T he next morning, Findlay arrived at his usual time of eight fifty-five precisely. He was amazed to see Todd sat on the step to his office.

"I see you, but I don't believe what I'm seeing! Whatever you want to talk about must be important?" He opened the door. "Come along," he said, "it can't be all that bad."

They made their way up the creaky wooden stairs to their office.

"Right," said Findlay, "first things first." And he lit the gas under the kettle.

"Now Sergeant, whatever brings you here at this time of day?"

Todd sat quietly, staring at the top of his desk. "It's Sally, sir."

"Yes?" said Findlay. "Is she ill?"

"No sir, nothing like that."

"Well? Spit it out. I don't have all day."

"Well, sir, I sort of proposed to her."

Findlay sat upright. "Good god, man, I nearly swallowed my tongue. I thought you said you had proposed to her."

"Yes," said Todd, "I think I did."

"What do mean, you think?"

"Well yes, I did. It all happened so fast. Before I knew what was happening, she was talking about telling everyone."

"Now you've had a chance to sleep on it. How do you feel?"

"I didn't do much sleeping," said Todd. "Every time I closed my eyes, I saw the vicar and the Torquay Building society. I can only just afford my digs at Mrs Bruce's; how will I afford an actual house?"

"Well," said Findlay, "you will have to stop visiting your posh friends in Exeter for a start. Oh, and no more fancy suits, and then there's the children, schools, clothing, uniforms, and not forgetting food and holidays. They eat lots and lots of food, every day they just keep on eating," said Findlay with a smirk.

Poor Todd looked terrified.

Findlay laughed. "I'm joking," he said. "Congratulations! Mrs F will be so happy when I tell her. She will say it's all down to her, of course, and I expect she will want to go shopping. Smile, Sergeant, why so glum?"

"I don't know, sir."

"Do you love her?"

"Oh yes, yes I do, very much."

"And she obviously loves you or she wouldn't have said yes."

Todd slowly nodded. "You're right, of course." He took a deep breath. "I'm a lucky man."

"Yes," said Findlay, "you are. Now Sergeant, the important stuff. The kettle has boiled, a little milk, no sugar."

Todd stood up to do the honours while Findlay sat back and began opening the morning mail.

"What's this?" he said. "It looks very official. It's stamped Ministry of Defence, and it's addressed to you, Sergeant."

"Me sir?" he said, taking it. He held it up to the light.

"What are you doing?" said Findlay. "Open it."

Todd ripped it open and began to read.

Findlay sat and waited.

Todd's face was suddenly very pale. He put the letter down and looked over at Findlay. "I'm called up, sir. It says the Devon constabulary has released me for active service, no need for us both in a small village in a time of impending war it says. Oh my god, I've got to go off and fight the Germans!"

Findlay was speechless. The two men sat quietly. Neither spoke for what seemed an age.

"I'll have a word at head office," said Findlay. "There has to be a mistake, you're no more a soldier or a fighter than I am. I'll speak to someone, get this put right, you're needed here."

"No," said Todd, "if my country needs me, then I must answer the call. There will be many young men like me, they won't be fighters either, and I expect they will be just as frightened as I feel at this moment, but to try and run away from my duty would make me a coward, and I'm no coward."

"No Sergeant, you're not, and I couldn't be prouder of you than I am right now."

Findlay was being a typical man. He could feel the sadness building inside him and he knew it was just a matter of time before he let his feelings overflow.

"There is one thing you haven't thought of."

"What's that sir?"

"You have to tell Sally and Mrs Bruce."

"Oh my god yes," said Todd. "Sir, I don't suppose you could?"

"Absolutely not," said Findlay. "This one is all yours."

He raised himself up from his seat. "Back In a jiffy," he said, and he left the room.

A few intakes of fresh morning air and his handkerchief to wipe his eyes did the trick. He was again in control and went back into his office.

"Right Sergeant, I have a mountain of paperwork to complete, plus the release forms for Mardie. It will be a long time before we hear any more about the Lady Preston. So, you have bad news to tell. Mrs Bruce and Sally need to know straight away. Did it say when you have to go?"

"The twenty second, sir."

"What?" said Findlay. "Of this month?"

"Yes," replied Todd.

"Then there's no time to lose. That's a little over three weeks away. I will finish up the Chelston Manor paperwork. You do what you have to do and meet me back at my house at four."

Todd smiled, "yes sir," he said, "four o'clock it is."

CHAPTER 25

L ater that day, Todd plucked up the courage to face the two women in his life; his landlady and his future wife. He decided to speak to Sally first. He stood under her bedroom window and gave one loud whistle. Sally appeared with the biggest smile he had ever seen. She ran downstairs, pulled open the side door and launched herself into his arms.

"What a lovely surprise!" she said. "I wasn't expecting you until later. Come on in, but my shift starts in an hour, so what can we do for an hour?" she mused, running her fingers through his hair.

Todd gave a faint smile.

Sally stared at him. "Please don't tell me you've had second thoughts?"

"Oh god no," he said, "nothing like that."

"Well, it's something," said Sally. "Here, sit over here. Allan, what on earth is wrong? If it's not me, is it work? Is it the inspector? Is he sick? Or are you sick?"

"Sally," said Todd, "stop talking. I have something to tell you. I wanted you to know before I go home and tell Mrs Bruce." Todd took her hand. He raised it to his lips and gently kissed it.

"Now you're frightening me," said Sally.

"I've had a letter," he said.

Sally shrugged her shoulders. "What kind of a letter?"

"It's from the Ministry of Defence. I've been called up."

Sally looked at him like a rabbit caught in headlights. "Called up?" she said.

"Yes, into the Army. I've got to go off and fight."

"Go off and fight who? Where?"

"Germany, I think, they didn't say. But probably Germany. Or maybe Poland, I don't know."

Sally sat quietly for a few seconds. Then she said, "You must ring them. Do it now. Tell them you can't go because we are getting married, and you don't want to fight anybody because you don't know them, and they've never done anything to you, and tell them you're a policeman!"

Todd smiled, "I wish I could, Sally, but I can't. I have to go. They are going to send me to a strange country I've only ever seen on maps, to fight people I don't even know. I'm terrified, Sal, absolutely terrified, but I have to do it."

Sally leaned forward, took his head in her hands, and kissed his forehead. "When do you have to go?"

"Three weeks. Just three weeks."

"Then I will have to let mum and dad know the wedding is off."

"Says who?" said Todd. "No Sally. Not off. Brought forward. As soon as possible, in fact. I'm not going off to some foreign land, leaving you here at the mercy of every single bloke in Torquay. No Sal, grab your coat. We are off to see the vicar. You'll be Mrs Sally Todd before you know it."

Findlay arrived home. He stopped at his front gate and sat and stared out of the car window. He knew there was nothing he could do to help Todd, and now he had to break the news to his wife. *She's not going to take this news well*, he thought. *She looked on Allan as the son she never had, she's going to be devastated. I'll need to get her on her own. Mardie has had enough worry, last thing she needs is to see us upset.*

He opened his front door to the usual greeting. "Hello dear, I'll be right there."

Findlay smiled, "I don't know what I would do if ever there was a time you weren't right there."

He glanced into the kitchen. Mrs F and Mardie were dicing up vegetables for the evening meal. "Do you have a moment, dear?"

"Yes, of course. I'm on my way," she replied.

She met Findlay in the hallway. "What is it, dear?" she asked.

Findlay opened the door into the best room. "In here," he said.

Mrs Findlay finished drying her hands and sat down. "Is everything alright, dear? I'm worried now."

"It's Allan, Allan Todd, he's been conscripted."

"He's been what, dear?" she said.

"Conscripted, called up. He's off to fight in the war effort."

Mrs Findlay sat quietly trying to take in what he had just told her. "Why?" she said. "Why would they take a young man like that and make him fight?"

Findlay could see the tears building in her eyes. He sat down beside her and put his arm around her. Nothing more was said, there was no need for more words.

"I've invited him round for tea," said Findlay eventually. "Four o'clock, if that's okay?"

Mrs Findlay lifted her apron and wiped her eyes. "That will be fine, dear. Yes, four o'clock is perfect. I will tell Mardie we are having company."

"How is she?" asked Findlay.

"Considering what she has been through, she's doing fine."

Findlay nodded. "Good he said, very good. She's actually a very bright girl. I need to go up to the Manor," he said. "They are finishing the excavations today. It will be interesting to see what else they have dug up in the last week. I'll be back by four dear. By the way," he said as he leaned over and kissed her, "dinner smells lovely." He smiled and closed the front door behind him.

CHAPTER 26

Todd and Sally arrived at Cockington Vicarage. Todd rang the bell, and they stood and waited, holding each other's hand. The vicarage door opened, and there stood Andrew Walsh; his family had overseen the religious beliefs of Cockington residents for generations. It was believed his family went back to the early eighteenth century.

"What can I do for you?" he asked.

He then raised his hand. "Stop," he said. "Let me guess. You've been called up, and he wants to get married as soon as possible?"

"Why yes," said Sally.

"You and the rest of Torquay. It seems most of the local boys have had the letter. How long do you have?" asked Reverend Walsh.

"A little under three weeks," said Todd.

"That's going to be cutting it fine. The bands have to be displayed on the church notice board for two weeks. That doesn't give you a lot of time."

"We know that," said Sally. "We can make it if you help us."

"Very well," said Reverend Walsh. "Come in and I'll get some details. The quicker we get the notice up, the better."

He took them through to the vestry. "Sit down please," he said.

Todd and Sally did as he instructed.

"Won't be long," he said. "Just need the right documents."
And he left the room.

Sally, still holding Todd's hand, looked at him with a smile.
"Are you alright, Allan?" she said quietly.

Todd whispered back, "I feel like I'm in the headmaster's
office, or getting it in the neck from Mrs Bruce for coming
in late."

They both sniggered.

"If he comes back with a long cane, I'm off! You'll be on
your own."

That started the laughing. They were both trying not to
laugh out loud, but it wasn't working. Sally could feel the
tears running down her face telling him to stop it, and Todd
sat blowing his nose.

"Shush," said Sally.

"Shush yourself, you started it!"

"I did not!" she said.

Suddenly the vestry door opened and reverend Walsh entered carrying a folder. "Right," he said, "let's get this done,
and you'll be pleased to see it's a simple folder, not a long
cane."

Sally and Todd looked at each other.

"There are no secrets in here," said the Reverend.

Sally gave Todd a gentle kick to the shin.

"Ouch!"

"Sorry, what?" said Reverend Walsh.

"Nothing," said Todd quickly, "a little bit of cramp."

Findlay arrived at the Manor. There were still a lot of
people in white coats milling around.

"Excuse me?" said a voice. "You can't be here. This is private property."

Findlay stood and stared. "And who might you be?" he said.

"Not that it's any of your business, but I'm Alicia Hammond. I'm the assistant coroner, and I say again you don't belong here. Please leave."

Findlay smiled. "Assistant coroner," he said under his breath. "Where might I find the actual coroner?"

"She's inside," she said.

"Could you please inform her that Detective Inspector Findlay is here to see her?"

"Oh, Inspector, I'm sorry I didn't know."

"No reason why you should, Miss Hammond."

"Please Inspector, call me Alicia. Ah, there she is."

Findlay looked over towards the Annex. "Beth," he shouted.

Beth gave a little wave and beckoned him over. He looked at Alicia. "I have to go now. The actual coroner is waiting for me," he said, pointing to Beth.

Alecia smiled. "Sarcasm is the lowest form of humour, Inspector."

"Yes," he said, "I know."

"Over here," said Beth.

She walked towards a small white tent that had been erected at the side of the Annex.

"What's this?" said Findlay.

"Seems we found the original doorway. They think the Manor at one time had an extra tower. This was a kind of priest hole. That's how they got all that treasure down there. It's actually very clever," she said.

"So, do they know what it's worth yet?"

"Not even close," said Beth. "I would normally log it and store it at my office, but this is huge. The British Museum is collecting it. Thank God I'm not responsible! So, Inspector, what brings you up here?"

"I take it you've heard Lady Victoria has been charged with Robert and Lord Preston's deaths?"

"Yes, I heard," she said. "That poor girl, the gardener, what was her name?"

"Mardie," said Findlay.

"Yes, Mardie, hard to believe anyone could knowingly take advantage like that."

"Yes, it is," said Findlay.

Beth stared at him. "Spit it out," she said. "I've known you long enough to know when something is bothering you."

"It's my sergeant, Allan Todd. He's been called up. Army, I think. He's got three weeks, then he has to go to Aldershot for training."

"Lots of young men have had that call," she said. "Why are you telling me this?"

"Because," said Findlay, "I don't want him to go. His job is here with me. I can't run half of Devon on my own. I know you have friends in high places. Can you pull any strings? Have a word in the right ear, maybe?"

"I see," said Beth. "Does he know what you're trying to do?"

"No, he doesn't," said Findlay, "and I want it to stay that way."

"I can have a word, but I can't promise you anything. I only have friends of friends. I don't have access to the Ministry of Defence or its ministers, but I will see what I can do."

"Thank you Beth," he said.

"Don't thank me," said Beth. "I haven't done anything yet. As I said, I can't promise you."

Findlay checked his watch. Three forty-five. *I better get home,* he thought. *Todd will be arriving in fifteen minutes.*

He climbed into his faithful old Volvo and made his way back to Cockington village. Todd arrived at the same time. He climbed out of his car. "Todd!" he shouted.

"Allan, I mean," he said with a smile. "Come on in, Mrs F has one of her famous stews cooking. She even had Mardie help with the vegetables. Come on in.

They walked into the kitchen. "Smells really good Mrs F," said Todd.

Mrs Findlay was standing at the kitchen sink. She spun around. "I didn't hear you come in," she said, wiping her hands on her pinny.

She outstretched her arms. "Allan," she said, "come over here, I need a hug."

Todd blushed as always, but quietly he loved it when Mrs F gave him a hug.

"I've told her about your call up, Allan. She's a little emotional."

"I'll be okay Mrs F, I'll be fine. I do have some other news for you, too."

Mrs Findlay took a step back and looked at him for a few seconds. "Oh my!" she gasped. "You're getting married?"

"Yes, I am," he said, laughing.

Todd looked at Findlay. "How does she do that?" he asked.

"Don't ask me," said Findlay. "I've never worked it out."

"Well, where's Sally? I take it, it's Sally you're marrying?"

"Well, it isn't Mrs Bruce," said Findlay.

"Sally had to work, but we spent the afternoon with the vicar. It's booked for the twenty-second of this month."

"That's just over two weeks. Oh, my word, two weeks to organise a wedding!"

"If anyone can do it, my love, you can," said Findlay.

"Don't forget," he said. "They have started rationing things. I wouldn't wait too long to get what you need."

"Just one other thing," said Todd. He turned to look at Findlay. "Will you be my best man?"

"Me!" exclaimed Findlay.

"Yes," said Todd. "You know I don't have any parents. I've always looked on you as a kind of father figure and Mrs F as the mum I never knew. Would you do it?"

Findlay took a deep breath, he straightened up and said, "I would be proud to be your best man Allan, very proud."

Findlay turned to Mrs F with a huge smile on his face. Mrs F was already crying into her pinny. "Come along, old girl," said Findlay, "wipe your eyes. Between the two of us, we will make this wedding a huge success."

Mardie put her arm around Mrs Findlay.

"I'll be fine," said Mrs F. "I'm hoping you will help me, Mardie. There's going to be a lot to do in the next two weeks."

"Yes please," said Mardie with a huge grin.

"That's the first time I've seen you smile," said Findlay. "You need to do a lot more of that. It's good for the soul."

"But for now, I'm starving. When do we eat?" said Findlay.

"As soon as you've washed your hands," she said. "Come along Allan, you can wash your hands in my kitchen sink."

"My, my, Allan," said Findlay, "you're highly honoured."

They finished their evening meal.

"That was delicious," said Todd. "Nobody does a stew the way you do."

"I'll agree with that," said Findlay.

They sat back in their seats and spent the evening chatting. The roaring log fire sparked and spat. The kitchen was warm and comfortable and still smelled of cooking. Todd could feel his eyes slowly starting to close.

"Is that the time?" he said. "I better get a move on. I told Sally I would be in before closing. Her shift finishes soon."

Todd stood up and put his top coat and gloves on. He thanked Mr and Mrs Findlay for the evening and put a hand on Mardie's shoulder. He gave her a peck on the cheek. "He is right, Mardie, smiling suits you."

At that, he said goodnight.

"Don't be late in the morning," said Findlay.

"I won't sir, I won't."

CHAPTER 27

T wo weeks flew by. The day of the wedding had arrived, and it was chaos in the Findlay household. Mrs Findlay and Mardie had performed a miracle. Everything that needed to be done had been done. The Findlay house was dressed for a reception and Findlay had decorated his pride and joy Volvo with ribbons and flowers. It was a crisp autumn morning, a slight mist floated over the fields and a bright sun lit up the sky with a beautiful coloured rainbow.

Todd was at the church along with the twenty guests invited by Mr and Mrs Findlay. He sat in the front pew bolt upright, waiting for his best man, who was also doubling up as father of the bride and driver.

Local handyman and plumber, Jim Heritage, hurried down the aisle. He leaned over to Todd and whispered, "she's arrived."

Todd could almost hear his heart beating. The vein in his neck started to throb, it always did when he was stressed.

Suddenly, Findlay appeared at his side. "Move up son, let an old man in."

Todd could feel the stress vanishing with every second now he wasn't waiting on his own.

The church organist, Elsie Bowden, who also doubled up at weddings, christenings, and funerals, began to play.

Todd's stare was transfixed on the altar. He turned to see Findlay still standing next to him.

"Sir," whispered Todd.

Findlay just stood with the biggest of smiles.

"Sir," said Todd again.

Findlay looked at him. "What?"

"Aren't you supposed to walk the bride down the aisle?"

The look on Findlay's face said it all.

"Oh hell, oh sorry lord, sorry, I mean, dash it!" He bent over hoping nobody would see him, and quickly tiptoed up the side aisle.

He had just arrived at the church doors when Sally and Mrs Findlay appeared. Findlay stood and stared, "Sally," he said with a whisper, "you look beautiful, absolutely beautiful."

"Thank you," she said. "I couldn't have done it without Mrs Findlay's and Mardie's help, and this wonderful wedding dress."

"It fits you better than it did me," said Mrs Findlay.

"Well go on," said Mrs F, turning to her husband.

"What? Go on, what?" said Findlay.

"You have to walk Sally down the aisle."

"Yes, of course, I know that," he said.

Mrs Bowden started to play the wedding march.

"Are you ready?" asked Findlay.

"As I'll ever be," she said with a smile.

Mrs Findlay straightened the knot in his tie. He pulled down his crisp white cuffs and offered Sally his arm.

Mrs Findlay gently pulled down her white lace veil, straightened out the back of her dress, then Mrs F gently kissed her on the cheek. "You're ready dear, go and get him." And she smiled.

They slowly walked down the centre aisle of Cockington Church, as hundreds had done before them. Cockington church had been in use for over a thousand years; ever since it was built by William de Falaise in 1069. Sally couldn't think of any church she would rather be married in.

They reached the altar. Todd turned to see his bride. He was overcome with the vision walking towards him and had to be steadied by his best man.

"You're beautiful," he whispered, "and you look amazing."

"I sincerely hope you're not talking to me, Sergeant," said Findlay and stepped back.

Sally gazed up at him. "I love you Allan," she said quietly.

He took her hand and just said, "and I love me too Sal, I mean you, I love you."

The Reverend Walsh came from behind the red vestry curtain. He smiled at both of them, then looked at Todd. "You're a very lucky man," he said.

The service began in the hushed church. Twenty or more people sat quietly and watched the joining of two hearts. Rings exchanged, the Reverend Walsh laid his hand upon theirs and said, "I now pronounce you man and wife."

Sally put her hand on Allan's cheek. They gazed into each other's eyes and she kissed her new husband. A round of applause echoed around the church while Mrs Findlay and Mrs Bruce sat wiping the tears from their eyes.

"Right," said Findlay. "It's all back to our house for drinks and a bite to eat."

Todd and his bride were standing holding hands and chatting to Sally's friend Joanne, and her husband Simon, when suddenly there was a huge flash of light, a blast of hot air, and an explosion that would make your ears bleed.

The whole congregation was thrown to the ground, and the church filled with black acrid smoke that felt like it was burning into their lungs. A German bomber on its way back from a raid on Plymouth had dumped its last remaining six-hundred-pound bomb.

It fell on Cockington village.

Whether it was on purpose or accidental; their aim couldn't have been more perfect. The bomb had landed in the rose garden at the rear of Cockington Court. The garden and the back of the Court took the worst of the blast, but the corner of the church where the bridal party had gathered was all but flattened.

The roof tiles had been ripped off and the two fourteenth century stained glass windows had been blown in. Glass and brick was scattered around the floor. Only the fact that the walls were built of Dartmoor granite stopped the whole building from collapsing.

"God help us!" cried Reverend Walsh. "Is everybody alright?" he shouted.

Findlay had fallen against Mrs F and had acted as a shield. The back of his body took the worst of it. "Are you all right darling?" he said, helping her to her feet.

"Yes, I think so. What about you?"

"Yes, I'm okay. What the hell just happened?" said Findlay. "Where's Allan, and where's Sally

Todd was on his knees at the back of the church. He was sitting quietly holding Sally's hand. Sally was laying among the brick plaster and glass, her beautiful wedding gown now stained with her blood from a wound to her head and chest.

Todd sat with tears running down his face. "It will be alright, Sal. Mrs F will sort this out. You'll be fine, my darling, just lay still until help arrives. Don't worry Sal. I won't leave you."

Findlay stood over him. All he could do was to look on in horror. He could see Sally was gone; she couldn't have survived such injuries. He bent over and took Sally's hand.

"Allan," he said quietly. "Allan, come with us. Come and sit over here."

"No!" he shouted. "I'll not leave my Sally like this. I'm staying with her.

"We will all stay with her," said Findlay. "Sit here Allan, you can still hold her hand."

Todd did as he was asked. He held on tightly to Sally's hand and just stared at her.

Findlay sat him down on a pew and Mrs Findlay sat next to him and took his hand in hers.

"Oh Allan," she said, "you're bleeding." She pressed her white handkerchief against a gash on the back of his head. "There are no words Allan, I am so, so, very sorry."

Todd just sat next to Sally and watched as Findlay and Jim Heritage helped members of the wedding party to their feet.

Todd simply wouldn't let go of Sally's hand. He went down on the ground again, "Sal," he said through his tears, "Sally, please wake up, please. Sal, just squeeze my hand." But there was nothing.

Todd came to the realisation that the love of his life had been snatched away. His Sally was gone. Todd put his face close to hers and sobbed uncontrollably. All Mrs Findlay could do was sit with one hand on his shoulder as she struggled to hold back her tears.

"We have to get everybody out," said Findlay. "I don't know how safe these walls are."

The Reverend Walsh came over. "It was a bomb," he said. "A German bomb. Why would you bomb a church? What kind of monsters would do this?"

The Reverend pointed to the corner of the church. "There are three more poor souls over there," he said to Findlay.

The explosion had raised the whole of Cockington and the villagers started arriving to see just what had happened.

Jim Heritage was an ex-Army officer, so had taken control. He was organising the men and stone by stone, clearing the mountain of granite.

Mrs Findlay's flower arranging club gathered on the Cockington green. They busied themselves helping the injured to safety and dressing wounds as best they could.

"I've rung Torbay hospital," said Mrs Bruce. "They said they will send everything they have."

"Wait," said Mrs Bruce, "where's Allan? And where's Sally? Oh god no!" she said. "Are they alright?"

"Allan is okay," said one of the ladies. "It's Sally, the bride. She was hit by some falling masonry. The word going around is that she has died, and there are another three bodies in the church. Jim Heritage won't let anybody up there. He said it was too dangerous."

Mrs Bruce just stared. "No!" she said. "Please God no. Not that lovely wee lassie, and on her wedding day! Where's Allan? I have to see him."

Mrs Findlay arrived. "Let the men do what they can," she said. "The best thing we can do is keep out of the way. I think help is on its way."

The bells of Torquay fire brigade could be heard in the distance. "It won't be long," said Mrs Findlay. "Allan is with Sally. He won't leave her. Best if we leave him alone for now."

Mrs Bruce couldn't hold back her emotions any longer and burst into tears. Mrs Findlay put an arm around her and just sat watching the village men digging furiously in the rubble. The emergency services arrived and began evacuating the injured while the ambulance service quietly took away the dead.

Todd was still sitting on the floor of the church, holding onto Sally's hand.

Two ambulance men stood over him. "Is this your wife?" asked one of them.

Todd looked up at him and nodded. The ambulance man went down on his knees and said,

"You don't want her laying in all this mess, son, surrounded by glass and dust. Let us help you, let us take her to the ambulance. You can stay with her until we reach the hospital. Come on lad, you will have to help us. Let's get her out of here."

Todd looked back at Sally. He gently caressed her forehead and nodded to the ambulance man.

"Good lad," he said. He motioned to his colleague. They gently lifted her onto a stretcher and covered her with a blanket.

"Ready?" said one of them. The other nodded, and they both lifted her up.

"Hold her hand, son," said one of the ambulance men, "you stay close to her."

They slowly climbed over the masonry and timbers scattered across the church floor and out into the sunlight. They made their way down the church path towards the waiting ambulance. The thirty or more men clearing the rubble stopped what they were doing. All that could be heard was the singing of birds. Each man removed his cap as Sally passed by.

The women on the green stood in silence and watched as they passed, with Todd still holding tightly to her hand. Mrs Bruce walked over to the ambulance and waited. They lifted Sally into the back. Mrs Bruce didn't say anything. She just squeezed Todd's arm as he climbed in with Sally.

CHAPTER 28

T he following morning, Findlay went to Mrs Bruce's lodging house. Mrs Bruce was standing on the front step. "Morning," said Findlay.

"Morning Inspector," she said. "I'm afraid he isn't here. He didn't come home last night. I can only hope he's still at the hospital."

"I'll go and see," said Findlay.

On arriving at the hospital, Findlay went directly to the front desk. "I'm Inspector Findlay, Cockington constabulary."

"Say no more, Inspector," said the receptionist. "The second floor has been kept open purely for the Cockington injured."

Findlay made his way up the stairs. He reached the ward and pushed open the doors. He recognised almost every person in there. Tom Small, the local Cockington milk farmer, came over to him.

"How could this happen?" he asked.

"I don't know Tom; I honestly don't know. Have you seen my sergeant?"

"I have. He's over there."

Findlay walked to a small private room at the end of the ward. Todd was sitting in a leather chair, staring out of the window. He looked so lost, so alone.

He pushed the door open. "Allan," he said. "You need to come home. Mrs Findlay and Mrs Bruce are so worried about you."

Todd didn't answer.

"Allan," he said again, "did you hear me?"

"It's my fault," said Todd. "If I hadn't asked her to marry me, she would still be alive."

"I understand you're hurting Allan, but you can't think that way. The plane that dropped the bomb had no idea where it was going to land. You can't stay here. Please Allan, come home with me."

"I have two days before I have to report to Aldershot barracks, but I won't be waiting. I'll leave today."

"No," said Findlay. "Allan, you can't. Come home with me. You will be staying with Mrs F and me at least for a couple of days. You're grieving, you're not thinking straight. Come to our house, just for a short while.

"I can't," said Todd. "I have to leave here, I have to go. I need you to look after Sally for me and explain to Mrs Bruce. My police salary will still be paid in, so my board will be covered. I have a little saved up, enough to pay for Sal's funeral."

"Of course," said Findlay, "but please reconsider."

Todd didn't reply. He just got up, shook Findlay's hand and said, "thank you for everything sir, and thank you for being my friend, I know Sally is in good hands, but I can't be here, I just can't and he walked out."

Findlay arrived home alone. Mrs F stood on the doorstep. "Where is he?" she asked.

"He's gone," he said. "He couldn't stay here. He asked if we could take care of Sally, I said of course."

Mrs Findlay nodded. "The village will take care of all those who lost their lives," she said. "Come in, dear. You need to get some rest."

CHAPTER 29

T odd arrived on the early bird train at Aldershot station. He stood in the middle of the platform, holding his brown leather suitcase.

The guard blew his whistle. "All clear," he shouted. The train slowly started to pick up speed as it spat out steam and smoke and left.

He made a very lonely figure standing alone on the platform in the half light of dawn.

He suddenly heard a voice say, "hello, are you going to the barracks by any chance?"

Todd just nodded.

"So am I," said the man, now walking towards him. "Would you mind if I join you? I thought for a minute there I was all on my own."

He was a short man of slim build, smartly dressed with a moustache and brylcreemed hair brushed back.

"My name's Andy," he said, holding out his hand. "Andrew Mann, and before you say it, I've heard it all before, Andy Mann, but I would rather you called me Andrew."

Todd just looked at him and said, "I wasn't going to say anything."

Andrew smiled. "What's yours?" he asked, still holding out his hand.

Todd ignored him and walked towards the exit. Andrew followed behind, pulling a very large oversized case behind him. When they reached the road, there was a ten tonne Army truck parked and waiting. Todd walked over to it and two uniformed soldiers climbed out.

"You boys for Aldershot?"

Todd nodded.

"What about your friend?" they said.

"He's not my friend," said Todd. "You'll have to ask him."

"Yes," shouted Andrew. "I'm for Aldershot."

"Well," said one of the men, "looks like it's just the two of you. Climb on the back."

Todd climbed up and lifted the cover to reveal two rows of metal bench seating. Todd set his case down and took his seat. He sat shivering in the early morning mist, but it didn't really matter to him anymore. He had already decided to leave everything up to fate.

Suddenly, the end of a case appeared under the tail cover of the truck. It was Andrew, trying to lift and push his suitcase on. Todd sat and watched him struggle.

"For God's sake!" said Todd.

He stood up and pulled the case on. A hand appeared through the cover.

"Please," said a voice.

Todd grabbed his hand and pulled.

"Thank you," said Andrew, "thank you. These things are not designed for people of five foot two."

He sat down next to Todd.

Todd stared at him. "There are seats on here for thirty men, and you sit next to me."

Andrew bit his bottom lip. "You're not very friendly, are you?" said Andrew.

Todd ignored him and edged his way along the seating, leaving a three-foot gap between them.

Andrew just sat and looked at him.

The truck engine started and set off for the barracks. About an hour passed and Todd could see a sign coming up. Southwood Camp. They had arrived just as the morning sun began to rise. The truck pulled into the main gates, being guarded by four soldiers with machine guns.

One of the guards waved them through and closed the barrier behind them. It was almost six o'clock. The camp was quiet, but just beginning to wake up. The truck stopped and the rear tail cover pulled aside. "Right, you two, out."

They climbed out and stood looking around them. The camp consisted of a few dozen long huts, each with up to forty men in each one, with a parade square in the middle.

"Right, you two," said a very officious looking man in a uniform. "You're in there," he said, pointing to one of the huts. "That will be home for the duration of your training. In one hour precisely, be back here and we will get you kitted out. Do you understand?"

Todd nodded.

"Have you no tongue, boy? It's yes sir. So, I'll say again, one hour back here, do you understand?"

"Yes sir," said Todd and Andrew quickly.

The man left them standing in front of the long hut. Todd walked up the steps carrying his case with Andrew behind struggling with his.

Todd pushed open the door. There were around fifteen beds on either side of the hut, with a tall metal locker at the side of each bed. There were men running around trying to get washed, shaved, and dressed.

Todd looked down at the side of the hut door. There were two empty beds on the mess plan.

"Oh, for god's sake," he muttered.

"That's handy," said Andrew. "We are neighbours."

Todd ignored him.

Andrew was trying to pull his case in through the doors.

"Oh, give it here," said Todd.

He grabbed the case and heaved it up onto his bed.

"Good god," said Todd, surprised at the weight of it. "What's in there?"

"Everything," said Andrew, "there's shortages of just about everything, so I will plug the gap. No matter what you want, I've got it. Well, almost everything." And he opened it.

Todd stood and looked. He couldn't believe what he was seeing.

"Where did you get all this stuff?" said Todd.

"Shops," said Andrew. "The Germans bomb them and all that stuff gets destroyed or pinched. So, I collect it and sell it on."

"So, you're a thief, a black marketeer?"

"Shush," said Andrew, "don't use words like that. I'm a businessman, a trader, anyone would think you were a copper," said Andrew.

Todd turned away and opened his case. There, folded neatly, starched and pressed, were his clothes. He lifted a shirt and there was a note.

It was from Mrs Bruce. It said,

My Dearest Allan.

I had a feeling you would do this, so I prepared some clothes for you, at least for a few days you will look presentable. Don't be a hero Allan, you come home to us in one piece.

They said on the radio that the war would be over by Christmas, so there will be a chair at the table for you. Here is some bread and cheese and I've wrapped your favourite for you, bread and butter pudding.

Take care dear boy, you are loved.

Todd could feel his eyes starting to well up and his nose starting to run. This was always a warning he was about to get emotional.

One of the men from the hut said, "Come along you two, get your kit stored away, don't want to miss breakfast, do you?"

They made their way to the canteen; an aircraft hangar, converted into a cafeteria come dining area for the soldiers.

Todd was stunned when he walked in and saw over a thousand men sitting having breakfast.

"Come on," said Andrew, "there will be nothing left."

They finished breakfast and waited outside their hut as instructed. The man in the uniform arrived exactly on time.

"Right, boys, your training starts now. My name is Connor, Sergeant Major Bill Connor. Sir, to you."

Todd smiled.

"Something funny lad?"

"No Sergeant, er, sir, nothing."

CHAPTER 30

Findlay arrived at his office at the usual time. He opened up and put the kettle on.

He sat waiting for it to boil, staring at Todd's desk. He was thinking about the day ahead. His first call had to be Cockington Church. When he left the night before, the village men had almost cleared the rubble. The Reverend Walsh was visiting the families of the bereaved and injured. Findlay couldn't help thinking how much worse it would have been had that bomb hit the church directly. The thought of him losing Mrs Findlay didn't bear thinking about. He could understand Sergeant Todd wanting to leave. Whether married thirty-five years or thirty-five minutes, the feeling of loss would break anybody's heart. It would be unbearable.

Just then, his office phone began ringing. Findlay picked it up.

"Cockington constabulary, Findlay speaking."

It was Beth, the coroner. "I've just heard your sergeant left."

"Yes, he did. His heart has been ripped out. Cockington is not the right place for him at this time."

"I'm releasing all four of the fatalities to their families. Under the circumstances, we can do away with formalities. You can instruct Mr Becket, the undertaker, as soon as he is ready."

"I see. Yes, I will do that Beth. My wife and I will be looking after Sally Todd."

"Will your sergeant be coming back for the funeral?"

"The truth is, Beth, I don't know. I don't even know if I can contact him. He's at an Army training camp in Hampshire, that's all I know, but as soon as I have a date, I will try."

"One other thing," said Beth, "the case against Lady Victoria Preston is to be heard on the sixth of November at Exeter high court. You'll get notification. Mardie will be called for the prosecution."

"Thank you, Beth," he said.

Findlay made his way to Cockington Church. The devastation was apparent as he drove along the path that led to it. He pulled up under an oak tree and climbed out. His first thought was all this carnage, and the old oak was still standing. For four hundred years, it had shaded the west wing of the church and not even a German bomb could move it.

Reverend Walsh came towards him. "Inspector, come, let me show you."

They walked to the top of the hill. A dozen or so of the local tradesmen were hard at work.

"What's going on?" asked Findlay.

"Every tradesman in Torquay has come to help; carpenters, thatchers, stonemasons, all giving their time and labour for free."

"That's wonderful Reverend, wonderful. How are the villagers holding up?" asked Findlay.

"As well as you would expect," he replied. "The first funeral is this Wednesday, Alice Gibbs. She was a friend of Sally's. She was married with two small children."

"Yes," said Findlay, "I know. Mrs Findlay and I will be there."

"Well, it's ten thirty Wednesday morning at the cemetery."

"I need to get home now," said Findlay. "My wife and I have to arrange Sally's funeral. We promised Allan Todd we would look after her, and look after her we will."

Findlay made his way home to collect Mrs F. They made their way to Torquay town and Becket's funeral services. He stopped outside and took a deep breath. Mrs Findlay took his hand. "Come along dear, this is for Sally and Allan."

Findlay nodded and pushed open the front door.

The funeral director, James Becket, was standing waiting for them.

"Inspector, Mrs Findlay, please take a seat. I saw you arrive," he said, "and I know why you are here. You are more than welcome to have an input, but it isn't necessary. Cockington parish is covering all four funerals and I will not be charging for our services. There's nothing to pay, nothing to organise. The funeral is this Thursday at ten."

"I see," said Findlay. He stood up. "Then we won't take any more of your time."

Mrs Findlay slowly got to her feet. "The flowers," she said. "May I do the flowers?"

"The ladies are waiting for you," said Becket. "Your flower arranging class is doing the display for both the church and for Sally. Just as soon as you get there, they are waiting for you."

Mrs Findlay smiled. "Come along dear."

"I'll drop you off," said Findlay.

They were walking back to his car when coming towards them was Simonds, Lord Preston's valet.

"Inspector," he said, "can I have a word?"

"You go ahead dear," said Mrs F. "I'll have a look around the shops until you're ready."

"Don't go far, dear. This will only take a few minutes," he said.

"Simonds, I can't imagine what you would have to say to me," said Findlay.

"It's about what Mardie said. I had nothing to do with the accident that killed her parents. It was such a long time ago, but I had nothing to do with it."

Findlay stood and glared at him. "The only person who could back you up is dead," said Findlay. "If you did or if you didn't, makes no difference now. Mardie is about to inherit the Preston fortune, and your job doesn't look too safe, does it? It's not me you have to convince. It's Mardie, and you're not her favourite person. Now if there's nothing else? I have more important things to deal with. "

CHAPTER 31

T odd had completed the third day of training when the whole camp was called to the parade square. Their commanding officer stood on the podium.

"Men," he said, "the German Army have taken Paris. France has fallen. It isn't difficult to see where Hitler's line of victories is heading. He's heading for Britain. The information coming out of Poland and France is not good. Atrocities are taking place on a daily basis. This will be the fate of our families unless we stop this madman at the French border. We need every man that can carry a rifle. Your training has been cut from six weeks to four days. We will be embarking for France this Friday. Those of you with family, you have three days to go home and see them. Every man will report back here by midnight this Thursday. Good luck to you all, dismissed."

The ranks of men began dispersing, and Todd slowly walked back to his hut.

"Looks like we are going to get to shoot some Germans, Toddy boy."

It was Andy Mann.

"I've told you, my name is Todd, not Toddy boy," he growled.

"So," said Andy, "you going home for a couple of days, see the wife, know what I mean?"

Todd didn't answer. He just went into the hut and slammed the door behind him.

Todd lay on his bed staring at the ceiling. Suddenly, the door burst open. It was Connor, Todd jumped to his feet.

Connor pointed at the half-dozen or so men who were busy packing their bags. "Give us five, lads."

They all left Connor and Todd alone in the Hut.

"Sit down," said Connor.

Todd sat down.

"We just had a phone call from a police officer in Devon, an Inspector Findlay."

Todd sat up on his bunk. "Findlay?" he said.

"Yes. I had heard about the church that was bombed; I had no idea it was you."

Todd didn't speak.

"That was rotten luck, lad," said Connor. "So now I know why you smiled when I said I was a sergeant. So, you're a copper? A sergeant at that. You kept that quiet. Probably just as well, with some of the sorts we have in here. Findlay said to tell you, your wife's funeral is tomorrow at ten. You better get a move on."

Todd just sat quietly and stared at the floor.

"You can't change what's happened, lad. I don't believe you're going to sit here feeling sorry for yourself when the woman you loved is about to be buried. You need to be with your wife, son. That inspector that rang has paid your train fare. Pack a bag, go see to your wife and be back here by midnight Thursday. We are shipping out to France."

Findlay was sitting at his kitchen table. Mrs F came in. "You look troubled, dear."

"I found out where Allan is, I rang them. They said they would pass on the message about the funeral. I bought his ticket. I'm hoping he will turn up by the morning."

"I'm sure he will," she said. "Sally was the love of his life. He won't let her down, you'll see." She kissed him on the forehead. "Don't worry," she said.

The following morning, Mrs Findlay was up and about early. "I have to go to the church, dear," she said. "We are putting the finishing touches to the floral display. The ladies and I have done her proud. It looks beautiful."

Findlay smiled. "Still no word from Allan," he said.

"There's time yet," said Mrs F, "it's early."

She put her coat on and walked the short distance to the church.

She pulled aside the plastic sheeting covering the doorway where the oak doors once stood.

As she walked in, she was almost overwhelmed by the smell of the hundreds of assorted flowers that adorned the walls and beams. It was then that she saw a solitary figure sitting on the front pew. She slowly walked down the centre aisle where just a few days before, Allan and Sally had walked on their special day.

"Allan?" she said, "Allan, is that you?"

She drew closer. It was him.

"Oh Allan, I knew you would come. I just knew it."

She sat down next to him and took his hand; he was very pale, she thought.

"I still can't believe it," he said. "We were going to do so much. I even made enquiries about buying the old police house next to Cockington Police station. Now it's all gone, and so is my Sally," he said.

He looked around the church. "They've started putting it back together," he said.

"Yes, everybody is helping, including the Drum inn. They have stepped in. They are up here several times a day with food and hot drinks. They closed the pub for a whole week out of respect for Sally. The whole village wants to help. We lost four of our own when that bomb was dropped. The village is one big family Allan. When one hurts, we all hurt. Let us help you through this."

Todd slowly nodded as he wiped away his tears.

"Come on, let's go home. Mr F is sitting waiting for news of you. Let's go and put his mind at rest. We still have two hours before the funeral. Yesterday was Alice's day. The whole village turned out for her. I'm sure today will be the same."

They made their way back to Findlay's cottage. Todd opened the front gate when he heard. "Hello Toddy boy." Over by the stream sitting on a rock was Andy Mann.

"What the hell are you doing here?"

"I asked the sergeant major where you were going. I said you would want me with you, us being such close friends and all that."

"We are not friends," barked Todd. "How many times do I have to tell you?"

"Hello," said Andy, holding out his hand to Mrs F, "I'm Andy, Andy Mann."

Mrs Findlay looked at Todd. "Is that really his name?" she asked.

"I'm afraid it is," he said.

"Come along Allan," she said. "Your friend has come a long way to be with you."

"He's not my friend," said Todd. "He's one of the blokes from the camp."

"How did you even get here?" said Todd.

"Train," he replied.

"You said you were skint."

"I am," said Andy. "I told them at the ticket office in Aldershot where I was coming. They had all heard about the bomb. They let me travel free. Like it or not, Toddy, you and me are mates. Where you go, I go," he said with a smile.

"In that case, Mr Mann," said Mrs F, "you'd better come in."

"Andrew, you can call me Andrew," he said with a smile, and I'm starving.

Findlay was overjoyed to see Todd. He shook his hand several times. "I am so pleased to see you Allan, I never doubted you wouldn't come."

Todd and Findlay sat in the best room talking. Todd was telling him about the impending embarkation to France.

Mrs F was in the kitchen with Andrew. "So how much do you know about the bomb?" she asked.

"Not much. He doesn't say a lot, to be honest. I can see he's troubled. I just don't know by what. He can push me away as much as he wants. I'm still his pal. I'm going nowhere."

Mrs F told him about the wedding and how he lost his love, and the bomb, and how four people lost their lives that day.

Mrs Findlay gave Andrew a cup of tea and a plate of her beef stew.

"So," asked Andrew, "how long have your husband and Toddy been friends?"

"Seven years," she replied, "but my husband was actually his boss until he was called up."

"His boss?" said Andrew.

"Yes," she said, "Mr Findlay is a Police Inspector. Allan was his sergeant, Sergeant Todd of Cockington Constabulary."

Andrew almost choked on his beef stew as he sat coughing and spluttering.

"Are you alright Andrew?"

"Yes," he said, putting his cup and saucer down. "I had no idea he was a policeman," he said nervously.

At that, Todd and Findlay came into the kitchen. "And who's this Allan?" asked Findlay.

"This is Andy, Andy Mann," said Todd.

Findlay looked at Todd.

"Before you ask, sir, yes, that's his real name."

"And what did you do before you were called up, Andy?" asked Findlay.

Todd quickly interjected, "probably best if you don't ask, sir."

"Oh, and why is that?" asked Findlay.

"I'm a trader, sir, a dealer in commodities."

"Oh," said Findlay, "you're a street dealer?"

"Well, yes, kind of," said Andy.

Mrs Findlay made them sit and eat an assortment of cheese and ham with salad.

"Wow," said Andrew, "I haven't had beef or cheese or ham for weeks with rationing. Where do you get it from?" he asked. "I think we could do a bit of business."

Todd gave him a look that, on a normal day, would kill.

Findlay looked at Todd, then the penny dropped. "Oh," he said, "now I understand what you do."

Mrs Findlay came into the kitchen wearing a long black coat and a black hat. "It's time," she said.

The three men all stood up together, and without saying a word, each put on their coats and hats.

Andy turned to Todd. "I would like to be there for you if you'll allow me," he said. "It's what mates do."

Todd said nothing, he just nodded.

They made their way up the hill to the church. It seemed as though the whole of Torquay were there to support him.

CHAPTER 32

The Reverend was waiting. When they reached the church, Todd turned to see crowds of people lining the lanes. "They'll have to wait outside," said the Reverend. "There's no more room in the church."

They made their way to the front pew, which had been kept empty for them.

"The service was beautiful," said Mrs F.

Todd nodded, and they made their way to the graveside and the internment began.

Mrs Findlay was holding a wreath.

"That looks like Sally's bridal bouquet," said Todd.

"It was," she said. "Sally so loved the flowers we used; I've used the same here."

Todd gave a little smile. "Thank you," he said.

She laid the wreath on top of the coffin. Todd fought back his emotions. He was afraid to let them go. Mr and Mrs Findlay stood on either side of him.

The service ended, and the crowds began to make their way home.

Todd turned to Findlay. "Can I have a little time for me and Sal?" he said.

"Of course, Allan. We will wait down the bottom for you."

Todd now stood as a lonely figure. Head bowed, he stared at Sally's coffin.

"That's it Sal, it's all over. I'm so, so, sorry. If I hadn't asked you to marry me, you would still be with us. This is all my fault. Now I will have to live with what I did. I'm off to France tomorrow Sal, me, going abroad. I've got to go fight the Germans. I don't think I'll be coming back, Sal, so keep an eye out for me. I'll be with you soon, and I'll take as many Germans as I can before they get me."

He threw a single tulip into the grave. "It's your favourite flower, Sal. I remembered. I've got to go now. I love you, Sally Todd, and I'll see you soon."

That evening, Mr and Mrs Findlay took Todd and Andy to the railway station.

"You take care Allan, don't go trying to be a hero. Your home, your friends, and your job will be waiting for you when you get back."

The train pulled out of the station, and they waved them off, not knowing if they would ever see him again. The following day, Todd and Andy were kitted out and before they knew it, they were on a troop ship heading for the French coast.

CHAPTER 33

The weeks passed, and no word was heard from Todd. Mrs F would call into the local post office every day to check if there was any post from overseas for her. "I'm afraid, not Mrs F," said the post mistress. "There's one here for the inspector."

"I'll take it for him," she said and made her way home.

Inspector Findlay was sitting at the kitchen table reading the morning paper. Mrs F came in through the back door. "Hello dear."

"Any news from Allan?" he asked.

"I'm afraid not, but there's one here for you. It looks official," she said.

Findlay was almost afraid to open it. He slowly removed the letter from the brown envelope and read its contents. He laid it on the table.

"What is it, dear?" she asked.

"It's Allan," said Findlay, "he's missing."

"What do they mean, missing?"

"It doesn't say, it just says he is missing. All avenues are being followed up to find his whereabouts, it says here. I guess we will have to wait and see, expect the worst and hope for the best," said Findlay.

CHAPTER 34

Another five weeks went by and still no word was heard about Todd until that Tuesday morning. They were woken by knocking on the door. Findlay jumped up and pulled on his dressing gown. He opened the front door and there stood Andy.

"I'm Andy Mann," he said, "remember me?"

"Of course I remember you," said Findlay. "Allan's friend, come in."

He showed him through to the kitchen, Mrs Findlay joined them.

"Andy," she said, "Oh god please don't tell us you're the bearer of bad news, please don't!"

"Just the opposite," he said. "Allan is alive! Injured but alive."

"Thank god!" said Mrs F, and she started to weep.

"Now, now, my love, don't upset yourself," said Findlay, putting his arm around her. "It's good news."

"I'm just sorry it's taken so long to get back," said Andy.

"You said injured. How injured?" asked Findlay. "And where?"

They all sat at the kitchen table and Andy began telling them the story.

"Our regiment was sent in to take a town called 'Arras' near the French coast. We were told it would be a piece of cake. When we got there, it was heavily fortified. The piece of cake turned out to be the first and third panzer divisions, the cream of the German Army. It was awful. Our lads were being cut to pieces. We were caught out in the open with no cover. All we could do was dig in and pray for reinforcements, but they didn't come. We were all terrified that the Germans would go around our flanks and cut us off. Some were even talking about surrendering. The machine gun and tank fire were continuous, day and night. I thought it wouldn't be long before they got us.

"Allan was very quiet, then suddenly he said he had an idea, but it was dangerous. Our captain said it couldn't be more dangerous than the pickle we were in. He said he did some tunnelling on a case he worked on here in Cockington."

Findlay smiled. "You could say that," he said.

"He got us to dig down into the sewers that ran under Arras. We moved an entire brigade through those tunnels and sewers. The Germans had no idea we were there or what hit them. They didn't see us coming. It was a brilliant idea, and it worked. We came up behind them in the dark, and the town of Arras was ours. Allan was hit by shrapnel. Got him in the back. He's in the Army medical unit in Aldershot. They are sending him home."

"When?" asked Mrs F.

"Today or tomorrow, I think. He was shipped out almost immediately. I believe he was on the missing list for a while. He's a blooming hero, he is. He saved the lives of a lot of men that night, including mine."

"Then I have to let Mrs Bruce know, and I better do some baking. He will need a good home cooked meal. Oh, and I'll make up the spare room for him."

"Slow down, dear," said Findlay, but she was too excited for slowing down.

Mrs Findlay put her arms around Andy. "Thank you," she said. "Thank you for letting us know!"

"Don't mention it," he said. "Toddy boy still won't admit he likes me, but we are friends. He can't fool me."

Findlay smiled. "Tell me Andy, does he allow you to call him 'Toddy boy?'"

"No, he hates it. I just like annoying him, it's the only fun I get these days." And he smiled.

Findlay put a hand on Andy's shoulder. "When did you last have egg and bacon?" he said.

Andy's eyes lit up. "I knew there was another reason for coming here! Are they black market?"

"Not quite," said Findlay, "our local butchers, actually. You're not in the city now. The very least we owe you is an egg and bacon fried breakfast."

"Lovely," said Andy.

Later that day there was a phone call from Torquay railway station. It was George Upton, the station master. "Just wanted you to know," he said, "your Sergeant Todd has arrived. We were going to drive him to you, but he insisted on going to the cemetery first."

"I will take it from here, George," he said, and thanked him.

"He's on his way, dear," said Findlay, "but his first stop is the cemetery."

"Then we will wait," she said. "Let him spend some time with Sally, we will be here when he's ready."

Todd was on two crutches. He stood quietly by Sally's grave.

"Hello my love," he said. "Can't believe I'm still alive. Those Germans tried everything to get me. I think I had an angel looking down on me, my guardian angel, Sally Todd. I've done my bit, they said. Whatever that meant, so I've been sent home. I'll be out of action for a while, but eventually I will heal and get back to work. It looks like you might have to wait a while for me, Sal, but eventually we will be together again. For now, I have to get on with my life, but you will always be a part of it."

Todd laid one single tulip on her grave and whispered, "I love you, Sally Todd."

Findlay drove slowly along the lane leading to the cemetery and stopped. Todd caught sight of him and gestured him over. Findlay drove to where he was standing and opened the passenger door. "Hello Allan," he said, "are you ready?"

Todd nodded and slowly eased his way into the car.

"It's good to have you back," said Findlay with a smile.

"It's good to be back, sir."

"I hear you're quite a hero?"

"Who told you that?" He stopped. "Don't tell me that annoying little man is here."

Findlay smiled. "Yes," he said, "he's here. I left him eating the last of my egg and bacon. I'm glad he came, Allan. He told us about your exploits. We have been so worried about you."

"I just need some rest," said Todd. "Please don't tell me he's staying with you?"

"Good heavens no," said Findlay. "Mardie has one room, Mrs F and I have the other, and you will be staying in the spare room. We are full!" said Findlay with a smile.

They arrived back at Findlay's cottage, Mrs F ran out and gave him the biggest of hugs.

"It's good to see you, Mrs F, very good."

"Your friend left. He said to tell you he will be back when you least expect him. He said he had to get back to the camp. He said he had customers waiting."

CHAPTER 35

The weeks passed by and Todd was healing. He had dispensed with his crutches and was coping with a single stick. Mrs Bruce was looking forward to him moving back home. Todd now had his routine. Every Sunday morning he would make the walk to get Findlay's paper and call at the cemetery with one single red tulip.

Findlay reported to his office each day at eight-thirty prompt, as he always had. He was going through some paperwork when his office door opened. It was Todd.

"I want to get back to work, sir."

"And I would be happy to have you back," said Findlay, "if you think you're ready? There's your desk, just as you left it. A mess," he said with a grin.

Todd sat down and started shuffling the piles of paper around.

"You're back just in time," said Findlay. "Tomorrow is the Preston trial."

"Poor Mardie," said Todd.

"I doubt she will sleep much tonight. What Victoria Preston tried to do was beyond disturbing; it seems money does corrupt, but we will worry about that tomorrow. For now, the Drum has been broken into. It's probably just the local kids, but we need to look into it. How do you feel about going back in there?"

Todd took a deep breath. "I have nothing but good memories, sir."

"If you're sure you're up to it, the Drum is all yours. Ease you back in gently," said Findlay.

Todd nodded. "I'll make my way down there now, sir."

"I will drive you."

"No, I'll walk. The exercise will help me heal, but thanks anyway."

Todd made his way down to the Drum. Findlay stood at his office window and watched him limp down the hill.

When he reached the Drum Inn, Todd stopped outside the doors and looked up at the single window that was Sally's room. For a few seconds he could hear her voice, then he thought he saw movement behind the curtains, but in his heart of hearts, he knew that was just wishful thinking. He was about to knock on the pub door when Findlay pulled up at the side of him.

"Get in," he shouted. "I've just had a call from Beth. The coroner's office has been broken into. They built a special vault there and were storing the gold and artefacts from the Manor, but it's all gone. The Drum will have to wait."

When they arrived at the coroner's office, Beth was standing with two colleagues and a small crowd that had gathered.

"Beth," he shouted, "what happened?"

"I don't know. I opened the doors and knew instantly things weren't right. It's all gone. They must have had transport. It couldn't be carried. The museum was supposed to be collecting it this morning."

"You're sure it wasn't them who took it?" said Todd.

"Not unless they have taken to breaking down doors," she said.

They walked around the inside of the offices. The doors were ripped off their hinges and the security vault was wide open. Todd picked up what was left of the vault lock. "I think your security needs upgrading," he said, holding the lock in the air.

"Nice to see you back on your feet, Sergeant," said Beth.

"Thanks," he replied. "Well, I would say it's probably being melted down as we speak."

"Most of it is worth more in its original form," she said. "Relic and antique collectors will want it untouched. But it's not that we should worry about, it's if it gets overseas, then it really will be gone."

"Let's get back to the office," said Findlay. "We need to contact the DCC ports at Plymouth and Exeter."

"What's a DCC?" asked Todd.

"Oh," said Findlay, climbing into his old Volvo, "it was introduced while you were away. It's the Devon and Cornwall Constabulary, that's what we are now called."

"What about Cockington constabulary?" said Todd.

"Gone," was the reply, "we are all now DCC."

"Good heavens," said Todd.

"It seems Cockington has become a centre of crime," said Beth. "The Drum and my office both broken into on the same night."

"That is strange," said Findlay. "If it were in the town, I could understand it, but not in the village. Well, Sergeant, the obvious place to look would be the Manor, but there's only Simonds there at the moment, Edward Preston is back in Exeter."

"There is no way Simonds could have moved that amount of gold on his own," said Todd, "let alone broken into the coroner's offices."

"We need to go up there, sergeant. Have a chat with Simonds. Then we need to drop in at the Drum. I have that feeling something isn't right."

Todd went quiet and just nodded.

CHAPTER 36

They made their way to Chelston Manor.

"Looks very different," said Todd.

There were overgrown gardens and pathways. The normally landscaped lawns looking more like neglected fields.

"You can tell Mardie isn't around," said Todd.

Findlay nodded. "She is almost ready to move back here," he said. "She was telling Mrs F it was time. I think she's waiting for the outcome of the trial tomorrow."

They walked towards the front of the Manor. Suddenly Simonds appeared carrying a shotgun.

"I sincerely hope that thing isn't loaded," said Findlay.

Simonds just stared. "What do you want?" he asked.

"Do you mind telling me where you were yesterday afternoon after five?"

"Not that it's any of your business, but I was here. I'm on my own, in case you've forgotten. Have you any idea how hard it is to look after a place this size?"

"One look around and we can see you're not coping," said Todd.

"So when can I expect the lady of the Manor to move in?" said Simonds sarcastically.

"I dare say she will let you know," replied Findlay.

Simmonds shook his head. "I know she has been staying with you and your wife. Has she mentioned me?"

"Not that I recall," said Findlay, "but I wouldn't be surprised if you were out of a job and a home by the end of the month."

"Inspector, do you honestly think that slip of a girl can run an estate like this? There are over three hundred acres of land, seven tenanted farms, plus the fishing lakes. Lord Preston struggled sometimes to cope. She has no experience, no idea how it works. She will destroy it."

"That slip of a girl," said Findlay, "is now one of the wealthiest young ladies in Devon. Even without the Preston gold, she is still very, very wealthy. You would do well to remember that. I'm sure anything she can't manage, she will employ someone to do it for her."

"You still haven't said why you're here?"

"The coroner's office," said Findlay. "It was broken into last night."

"The Preston treasure," said Simonds, "don't tell me it's gone."

"That's exactly what I was going to say," said Todd, "but of course you wouldn't know anything about that, would you?"

Simonds glared at them. "No, I would not," he replied.

"Very well," said Findlay. "I will need to speak to you again. Come along sergeant, let's not keep Mr Simonds from his work."

They made their way back to the village. "If you are sure you're up to it, Sergeant, we need to go to the Drum."

"I'll be fine sir," said Todd. "Just fine."

They arrived at the Drum just as the doors were opening. "Morning boys," said Greg Stephens, the new landlord.

"Morning," said Todd inquisitively. "Where's Dave Morgan?"

"He's gone," said Greg. "Not long after the bombing of the church, he just packed up and left. I've just taken over; I reckon he was having a thing with the barmaid that was killed. I reckon he was heartbroken," he said with a smile. "She was getting married on the day the bomb dropped. I don't think he was happy about the marriage."

Todd stood and glared at him. "What did you just say?" asked Todd.

Findlay quickly stepped in between them. "And who told you that, may I ask? Or are you just making it up as you go along for conversation? You are on very dangerous ground."

Stephens looked at Findlay, then at Todd. "Just what I hear over the bar. I wouldn't know, not really," he said. "Hell," he mumbled, "is your name Allan Todd?"

Findlay again stepped in.

"I suggest you get behind the bar, Mr Stephens, before I let my sergeant loose."

"Allan, sit over there. Mr Stephens here will bring us a pot of tea, won't you? Then I have some questions for you."

"Yes, of course sir, Inspector sir, right away," and he disappeared into the kitchen.

"Why would he say that?" asked Todd.

"It's small minded village tittle tattle, take no notice of him. Every village has its idiot. It looks like ours was imported from Exeter. Ignore him."

Todd nodded.

Findlay and Todd sat in the corner booth. "This is where I proposed to Sally," he said.

Findlay didn't say anything.

Todd smiled. "She was so happy, so excited. I can hear her now," he said.

"It's going to take a long time," said Findlay. "Everywhere you go there will be memories."

"I don't think I ever heard you and Sally argue," he said.

"We didn't, sir, not really. I loved her. Nothing she could ever have done would make me argue with her, nothing. As for what that idiot just said, he's lucky I didn't knock his block off."

"Self-control, Sergeant, consideration and self-control, that's what makes you a good policeman."

Stephens appeared carrying a tray of tea. He placed it on the table in front of Todd and sat down. "I'm sorry," he said to Todd. "I should learn to keep my mouth shut."

Todd just looked at him. "That could be a good idea," he said.

"You reported a burglary?" said Findlay.

"Yes, I did. It wasn't so much a burglary," said Stephens, "more just a break in. They didn't take anything."

"Why would you break into a pub and not take anything?" said Findlay.

"There's nothing here of any value," replied Stephens. "I have a room in Chelston. Nobody lives here now. It's a lock up pub. The takings come home with me at nights."

"So, when you finish at nights you lock up and go home?" asked Todd.

"Yes," he replied.

Todd raised his eyebrows and sat back in his seat.

"Is something wrong, Sergeant?" asked Findlay.

"I don't know, sir. When I arrived, I was sure I saw somebody at the window in Sally's old room. I put it down to my imagination, but now I'm wondering if I was right?"

"I can assure you," said Stephens, "there's nobody here. In fact, the door leading to the upstairs rooms is locked. The key is missing. I'm waiting for the brewery to send me a replacement."

"Well," said Todd, "I can only tell you what I think I saw."

"That's good enough for me," said Findlay, standing up. "Come along, Sergeant, we need your muscles. "

Todd leaned against the door and pushed. Findlay leaned over and also pushed against the lock. Suddenly, the door sprung open and slammed against the hallway wall.

Findlay leaned in and looked up the stairwell. "Looks quiet enough," he said.

The three men made their way up the stairs. When they reached the top, Todd stood outside the door leading to Sally's room.

"Are you alright?" asked Findlay.

Todd just nodded and pushed open the door. "The smell of her perfume is still here," said Todd, taking a deep breath, even after all this time. He walked in and went over to the window.

"It looks quiet enough," said Stephens.

Todd nodded.

"I'll check the other rooms," said Stephens and left Todd and Findlay alone.

Todd sat on the single bed and ran his hand over the top quilt.

"Come along, Sergeant," said Findlay.

Todd stood up and walked towards the door. Suddenly, he stopped dead.

"What is it?" asked Findlay.

"Maybe nothing," he replied.

Todd was staring at the oak panel on the inner wall. "One thing about Sally," he said, "she was fastidious about cleanliness. She kept everything spotless."

Todd bent down on one knee. "Look at this," he said.

Findlay bent over.

"What's that?" asked Todd, pointing to a dust print between the floor and panel.

Findlay bent down and rubbed it. "It looks like dried mud," he said.

Todd stood up and stared at it. "It looks to me like part of a heel print," said Todd.

Findlay started pushing on the panelled wall, "just out of curiosity," he said.

He pushed on the corner panel and, to their amazement, the entire panel opened in front of them.

"Good god!" said Findlay. "It's a priest hole."

"A what, sir?"

"A priest hole," he said. "During the reformation, the priests used them to hide from the king's inquisitors and to hide valuables."

"Mr Stephens!" shouted Findlay. "A torch, if you please, a large one."

Stephens ran down the stairs and returned with a torch.

Findlay shone it into the blackness of the recess. "Very strange," said Findlay. "They are usually just big enough to hide a couple of men. This one seems to go down."

He stepped inside. "There's a ladder here," said Findlay. "It looks like it's just been put here recently. It certainly isn't five hundred years old. Hold this," he said, passing the torch to Todd.

Findlay began climbing down, "some light sergeant please."

Todd aimed the torch light down into the darkness. "Careful sir," said Todd.

Findlay was about twenty feet down when he touched the ground.

"Sergeant!" he shouted. "Come down."

Todd made the climb to the bottom.

"Well, I never," said Findlay. "It's a tunnel."

"I wonder where it goes?" said Todd.

"Only one way to find out, Sergeant."

They slowly made their way along the winding tunnel, which seemed to go on forever. Suddenly, they reached a fork.

"Which way, sir?" asked Todd.

Findlay shook his head. "No idea. Left is as good a path as any."

They steadily made their way further down the tunnel. After a while Todd said, "look sir, light. It's a doorway," he whispered.

They turned off the torch and stood silently, just listening. "I can't hear anything, sir."

"Neither can I," said Findlay. He reached for the handle and was about to turn it when Todd grabbed his arm.

"Listen sir," he said, "I can hear voices."

"Can you hear what's being said?" whispered Findlay.

"No sir, it's a man and a woman, that much I can hear."

Findlay very slowly started turning the handle. Both men stood with bated breath, waiting to see what was on the other side of the door.

Findlay again slowly pulled on the handle, the door unlocked and Findlay put his eye against the crack. "Good god," he whispered.

"Sir, what is it? What's there?"

Findlay slowly opened the door. The two were suddenly bathed in light and there, standing in front of them looking dumbfounded with shock, was Beth the coroner, and her assistant.

Findlay and Todd walked through the door and into her office. "What's going on?" said Beth. "How did you get here?"

Todd closed the door. "It's a wall panel," he said. "You would never guess it was a door. I think you need to do some explaining, don't you?"

Findlay leaned up against the desk and stared at the wall panel. "Well," he said. "Now we know how they moved the gold and artefacts. It was dragged along the tunnels that lead to the Drum, which explains the ladder."

"What ladder?" asked Beth. "What tunnels and where did you come from?"

Findlay told her of the priest hole and the tunnels which ran all the way from the Drum to her office. "I see," said Beth. "I don't know much about this building, but I do know it used to be the home of the Arch Deacon back in sixteen something or other."

"That would explain it," said Findlay, "which begs the question, where does that second tunnel lead?"

"I'm betting it goes to the Manor," said Todd. "That thought occurs, but until we check it out, we won't know."

Todd pulled on the panel. It wouldn't budge.

"It's a one-way, Sergeant. It's been a secret door for four or five hundred years. It will still be there tomorrow. We will have to get entry from the Drum or remove this wall panel. I think the Drum is a better way."

"Yes," said Beth, "it certainly is."

"Whoever took the Cockington treasure didn't do it alone. I have a feeling the other tunnel will lead us to whoever is responsible. Tomorrow is the trial of Lady Preston. I want you there Todd," said Findlay. "I doubt Mardie will attend until she is called to give evidence. I need to know everything that happens."

"Yes sir," said Todd.

CHAPTER 37

T he following day, Sergeant Todd arrived at Exeter crown court and made himself known to the prosecution lawyer. "Hello, my name is Todd," he said.

The prosecution lawyer turned around. She smiled. "Hello, my name is Alison, Alison Thomas. You must be Allan Todd from Cockington? I've been expecting you."

Todd stood and stared; he couldn't believe what he was seeing. Apart from the hair colour, it was like looking at his Sally.

She held out her hand. "Pleased to meet you," she said.

Todd shook it, and simply said, "Hello."

He couldn't get over the likeness to Sally. He didn't know if he should be excited or confused, or if he should even still be in the same room as her. Every fibre of his being said leave, but he just couldn't.

"So, Sergeant. It is Sergeant, isn't it?"

"Yes, yes, it is," said Todd.

"So, I understand you were there when Lady Preston made her confession?"

"Yes, I was," said Todd.

"We have your statement, so it's unlikely you will be called, unless, of course, she puts in a not guilty plea."

"Is that likely?" asked Todd.

"No, not really. She's been informed that if she wastes the court's time, her sentencing will go badly for her."

"What about the gardener, Mardie?" asked Todd.

"Again, Sergeant, it depends on her plea. She may have to give evidence, or maybe not. We will know later today."

At that, Alison turned and walked towards the courtroom. Todd stood and stared, then sat down to catch his breath. He could feel his heart thumping in his chest. His mouth was dry and his hands were shaking. He took out his handkerchief and wiped his forehead.

Suddenly the door opened and in walked Findlay. "Sir," said Todd, "I wasn't expecting you to come."

"I wouldn't miss this for the world, Sergeant. She deserves everything she gets."

Findlay stood and looked at him. "Sergeant, what on earth is wrong? You look like you've seen a ghost."

"You're not far wrong, sir." Todd told him about his meeting and the uncanny resemblance to his Sally.

Findlay stood up. "Wait there, Sergeant, I have to see this lady for myself."

Findlay crossed the hallway and entered the courtroom. A few moments later, he came out and walked over to Todd.

"Good heavens," he said, "if I had known I would not have sent you here, the resemblance is amazing. Apart from her hair, she does look remarkably similar. Come, Sergeant, sitting around here will do you no good. I'll leave our contact details. If they need us, they will find us."

All that day Todd couldn't get her out of his mind. He sat in the lounge of the Grand Hotel, forcing himself not to go back to the courthouse. Findlay ordered afternoon tea and sat down opposite Todd. "You're very quiet," he said.

"I'm sorry, sir."

"Don't apologise, Sergeant. I can understand how you must be feeling. I must admit, the resemblance was quite unnerving."

Todd said nothing.

"It's been over a year since we lost Sally," said Findlay. "Your injuries have healed. Maybe it's time you started getting out a bit more."

Todd shook his head, "I don't think so, sir. I found my soulmate in Sally. I'll never get that again."

"Not if you stay locked up in Mrs Bruce's lodging house or our office, you won't. Sally wouldn't want you becoming a recluse. You were both too full of life for that. If you like this girl..."

"Alison sir, Alison Thomas."

"Alison," said Findlay. "It's time you met people your own age. Ask her out for a drink."

"I'll think about it, sir. Maybe I will."

Findlay lifted the tea pot and began pouring. He suddenly stopped. "Sergeant," he said, "do you believe in fate? Look behind you."

Todd turned around to see Alison Thomas standing at the bar with what looked like a barrister in full gown.

She glanced over and smiled. "Excuse me," she said to her colleague.

"Well, well, Sergeant Todd, and who is this?"

"This is my boss," said Todd, "Inspector Findlay."

She outstretched her arm. "Pleased to meet you, Inspector."

"And a good afternoon to you," said Findlay. "Actually, I was just leaving," and he stood up. "Perhaps you and my sergeant could manage a pot of Indian tea?"

"Sir," said Todd in a panic.

"No need to thank me," said Findlay." It's just a pot of tea." Findlay smiled. "I'll see you in the morning, eight-thirty sharp." And he left.

"Should I be mother?" she said.

"Pardon?" said Todd.

"Should I pour?"

"Yes, please," said Todd, "please do."

She poured the tea and sat back in her seat. Nothing was said for what seemed an age.

"Tell me, Sergeant, do I make you nervous? You seem on edge."

"No," said Todd, "not really, well, maybe a little."

"I couldn't help but notice you kept staring at me," she said.

"Did I?" said Todd, "I apologise, sorry."

"It's not a problem, Sergeant. I can't keep calling you Sergeant. What's your first name?"

He was about to say, "Allan." When she said, "no, no, don't tell me, I'm good at this. Your first name is Jack?"

Todd shook his head.

"Okay," she said, "Steven?"

Todd again shook his head.

"Well, you look like a Steven," she quipped.

"It's Allan, my name is Allan."

"Yes, I know," she said with a smile. "Now do you feel more comfortable?"

Todd smiled. "That was very cruel," he said, and they both laughed.

"It's my job to know who I'm dealing with," she said. "There's no need for you to tell me anything. I already know who you are, where you come from, and what happened to you. It was an awful, awful thing, and I hope eventually you will get over your broken heart."

After a pause, she said, "So, Allan, let us start again. Hello! My name is Alison."

She held out her hand. Todd took it. "And I'm Allan," he said.

"It's a pleasure to meet you, Allan. Now drink your tea before it goes cold."

They both smiled.

"So," said Todd. "Did Lady Preston plead?"

"Yes, she did," said Alison. "Guilty. It's pretty much a closed case. She admitted her guilt. It was all for money."

"So will we have to attend the court?"

"No," she said, "not now. You can let that young woman, Mardie, know it's all but over. The law will deal with her now."

"I'm glad about that. Mardie is such an inoffensive girl. The way that family treated her was quite shocking. And then trying to get her to take the blame went beyond all boundaries."

"You're quite a passionate soul, aren't you, Allan?"

Todd could feel his face starting to turn crimson as he shuffled uncomfortably in his seat. "I apologise. I do tend to say what I think."

Todd stared at her hand on his. It was as if he had just received an electric shock. He felt his stomach churn and his mouth go dry.

She let his hand go. "I must get back," she said. "Before I go, Allan, I would like to see you again if you're agreeable?"

Todd nodded.

"Good," she said, "I will ring you."

CHAPTER 38

The following morning, Findlay was in his office at eight-thirty on the dot. Nine o'clock came and still no Todd. Findlay stood at his office window wondering where his sergeant was when he saw him walking down Cockington Lane, coming from the woodland cemetery.

Findlay sat down behind his desk and waited for him to arrive. He heard Todd climbing the wooden staircase, so he picked up his newspaper.

Todd walked in and sat down behind his desk.

"Morning, Sergeant."

"Morning sir," said Todd. "Sorry I'm late sir, I've been up to visit Sally."

Findlay put his paper down and took a deep breath. "All right, Sergeant, what's going on? And what happened after I left the Grand yesterday?"

"I'm not sure, sir. We sat and we talked, and she said she wanted to see me again."

"Excellent," said Findlay. "So why are you looking so glum?"

"Well sir, I said I would, then I thought about it. I can't do it. I can't see anybody else. So I went for a chat. I told Sally all about her."

"And?" said Findlay.

"And nothing sir. It just doesn't feel right."

"So when will it feel right?" asked Findlay. "One year? Two years? Three? If this young lady likes you enough to want to see you again, you're a very lucky man. "

Todd bit his bottom lip. "That's what the vicar said to me on our wedding day, 'you're a very lucky man,' I wasn't that lucky, was I?"

"Suppose it was you who had died that day?" said Findlay. "Would you begrudge Sally happiness? Would you want her to meet someone that might make her happy? Of course you would, and she would want the same for you, because she loved you. I would give it some serious thought before you close that door, Sergeant."

Nothing was said for several minutes.

Then Todd said, "Lady Victoria pleaded guilty."

"I know," said Findlay. "She's to be sentenced next week. Right, Sergeant, we have a tunnel to explore. We will go in from the Drum end. I don't think our coroner was very happy about having her office walls torn down."

Findlay picked up two heavy duty torches and passed one to Todd.

Todd smiled. "Now this is what I call a torch. Don't break it, Sergeant, it's on loan from our home guard."

They made their way to the Drum where the landlord, Stephens, was waiting for them.

They climbed down the ladder into the blackness and turned on the torches.

"Slowly does it, Sergeant," said Findlay as they crouched down and made their way along the tunnel.

It wasn't long before they reached the section where they had turned left the day before. Findlay held his torch out and peered into the blackness.

"Well," he said, "we've come this far."

They made their way along the narrow tunnel as it twisted and turned. Suddenly, they came to a dead end. "That's as far as we go," said Todd, "and look, another ladder."

Findlay pointed his torch upwards. "A trap door," he whispered. "Right, Sergeant, up you go, quietly."

Todd slowly climbed the ladder until he reached the top. He reached up and pushed on the wooden hatch. It moved a little. "I think there's something on it sir, it's heavy."

"Try again," whispered Findlay.

Todd put his shoulder to it and, with all his strength, he pushed. The hatchway suddenly gave way and whatever was standing on it fell over with a crash.

Findlay closed his eyes and slowly shook his head. He looked up at Todd. "Could you make any more noise, Sergeant?" He said quietly.

"Sorry sir, I couldn't help it." Todd slowly put his head through the opening. He raised his torch and shone it around the room.

"Sir!" he shouted. "It's here, the gold from the coroner's office, it's all here!"

He climbed up and into the room. Findlay appeared after him, "give me a hand sergeant," he asked.

Todd pulled him up through the hatch. They both shone their torches around.

"Good heavens!" said Findlay. "I had no idea there was this much of it. The question now is, who took it, and where are we?"

"Over there, sir. A door," said Todd.

They slowly walked over to the door. Findlay shone his torch on the floor. There was a barrel laying on its side with gold artefacts lying around it. "I'm impressed, Sergeant," said Findlay, "you lifted that, you're obviously fit again."

"Over here, sir."

Todd pulled a large brown sack into the middle of the room and tipped its contents out. Solid gold plates, goblets, and religious artefacts fell to the floor.

Finlay opened a wooden box and just stared at it. "Look at this," he whispered.

The box was full of gemstones and coins of gold and silver. "There must be a million pounds here," said Todd.

"There's a lot more than that," said Findlay.

They reach the door. Findlay took hold of the handle.

"I'm half expecting Simonds to be on the other side," said Todd.

Findlay opened it just enough to see through. "Wherever that tunnel comes out, Sergeant, I don't think it's the Manor. Have a look."

Findlay stepped back and Todd peered through the crack. "Oh my god," he said, "it's a cave."

He opened the door wide enough to get his hand through and shone his torch around. "I don't think anyone is here, sir."

They walked through and into a small cavern.

Todd looked down. "Sand, sir," he said, "and it's dry. At least we won't drown."

"Whoever they are, they have been here recently." Findlay pointed his torch to the ground. "Footprints, Sergeant, I don't think we are alone."

"Look over there," said Findlay, "the cave entrance."

They walked through the deep sand and Todd looked through the opening. "It's Oddicombe cove sir."

Findlay stood for a moment. "So the tunnel running to the coroner's office is from the priest hole at the Drum. If I'm not mistaken, this is an old smuggler's tunnel leading to the sea. At some point in history, the two were connected."

"We have the Cockington gold," said Todd, "but not who took it."

"We won't have it long if we leave it here," said Findlay. "I have a feeling they haven't gone far. Hold the sack," he said and Findlay began dropping the artefacts into it.

Todd dragged the sack over to the hatchway.

"Listen," said Findlay, "can you hear that?"

Todd stood motionless and tried to listen over the sound of the waves on the rocks below the cave entrance. "It's an engine, sir, a boat."

Todd dropped the sack through the hatch, which landed with a crash at the bottom. He ran over to the cave entrance and peered around the rock face. "It is," he said. "It's a boat, and I think I saw four men in it."

"Now what do we do?" said Findlay.

"It's two each, sir."

"What?" said Findlay.

"Two each sir, I'm sure we could handle them!"

"Sergeant, look at me, do I look like a heavyweight boxer?"

"Then we hide," said Todd. "We can go behind the rocks in the dark. At least we will be able to see what we are up against." That's better than a fight said Findlay.

They quickly went behind the rocks and waited.

Suddenly, they could hear voices. "German," whispered Findlay, "that's German."

The voices got closer until they were in the cavern. Findlay and Todd just stared at each other. "I have to get a look at them," whispered Findlay. He slowly moved around the rocks until he could focus on whoever was there.

Findlay peered around the rock and strained to see through the gloom of the cavern. His eyes slowly became accustomed to the dark. He could clearly make out four men. Two were bagging up the gold while the other two had their backs to him and stood talking.

"Sir," said Todd, "sir."

"Shush, Sergeant, wait."

Suddenly, the two men turned around, the one with the torch was shining it around the floor.

Findlay moved back into the darkness. He stood for a few seconds then said, "oh my god, it's Oswald Mosley."

"Who?" said Todd.

"Mosley, he's the leader of a fascist organisation. I saw him at Speakers' Corner once, an impressive man to listen to, but a traitor."

Todd peered around the rock face. "Sir," he said, "the man with him, it's Edward Preston."

"Of course," said Findlay, "now it all fits. I did some checking on Preston. He's got quite a reputation in Exeter. The word is that he's some kind of fascist agitator. That explains why he left as quickly as he did and why he did not question Mardie being next in line. He knew he would have all this. We can only presume this gold is on its way to support the German war effort."

The two men dragged one of the sacks to the cave entrance, tied it with rope, and lowered it down to the beach below.

Todd couldn't help himself. He saw an opportunity to half the threat. He ran as best he could across the deep sand towards the two men standing on the cavern edge. They turned around just as Todd reached them, but they were too late.

Todd barged into them and sent them both plummeting to the rocks below. Mosley and Preston made a grab for him, but right behind them was Findlay.

"Hands up!" he shouted, "Or I shoot!" as he pushed his pipe into Mosley's back. "Make no mistake, gentlemen, I will shoot you. Now down on your knees, both of you."

"Sergeant, take off your tie and belt, tie them together."

Todd removed his tie and belt and secured both men together in a sitting position.

"Now Sergeant, there's a public phone box at the top of the hill. Please call for assistance. I will keep an eye on these two traitorous miscreants."

"Right away, sir," he said, and left.

Findlay was still standing in the shadows of the cave holding out his pipe. "Try anything funny," he said, "and I will take great pleasure in shooting you dead. Do you understand?"

"Yes," they replied.

They sat quietly until Edward Preston said, "I didn't know Cockington police were armed."

"Then think again," said Findlay.

Mosley turned his head and looked directly at Findlay. "Do you know who I am?"

Findlay didn't answer him.

"When my followers find out who you are, they will be here looking for you."

Findlay still said nothing. He was too busy watching the cave entrance hoping help would arrive quickly and praying they didn't realise he was holding them, not at gunpoint, but pipe point.

"A bag full," said Preston.

"What?"

"I said a bag full. Enough gold to let you live like a king. You can help yourself. Just untie us and it's yours."

"I'm thinking I should just shoot you now," said Findlay.

Suddenly, Mosley began wriggling and swaying from side to side. With one pull, his hands were free. He slowly stood up while rubbing his wrists. "Well," he said, "are you going to shoot me, or should I just offer you a match?"

"What are you talking about?" said Preston.

"Get up Edward, he's not going to shoot anybody, at least not with a pipe he isn't."

Findlay took a deep breath and lowered his arm. He took out his matches and lit his pipe.

"You almost had us," said Mosley, "standing in the shadows was a good idea, but when the sun moves so does the shadow, there isn't much light in here, but there's enough for me to see it was a pipe you were holding. Very brave of you." Mosley put his hand into his pocket. "Now this," he said, "is a real gun."

He pulled out a German Luger pistol and cocked it. "I should shoot you where you stand," he said. "They were two of my best men your sergeant just threw down onto the rocks. But I'm no fool. Shooting a policeman is certain to lead to the gallows if I get caught. You are going to help Edward here to fill up the bags. Then you are going to help him carry them to the boat. Off you go, Inspector."

Findlay thought it best to do as instructed. Help would be here soon, he thought.

Todd had called for help. Officers were on their way and Todd was running back down the hill towards the cove, when in the distance he saw a truck winding its way towards Cockington Village.

He stood panting with his hand shielding his eyes from the sun. "It's an Army truck," he thought. He ran as fast as he could over the fields towards the road, waving his arms around.

The truck skidded to a halt. Todd stopped some fifty feet in front of it. Suddenly, the passenger door opened and a uniformed soldier jumped out. "Toddy boy!" shouted a familiar voice.

"I don't believe it," said Todd. "Andy Mann, I've never been so pleased to see anyone."

"Toddy boy, whatever is wrong?"

Todd told him what had been going on. "I need help," he said. "I've left the Inspector holding them at gunpoint using his pipe as a pretend gun."

"I think I can help with that Toddy boy!" He went to the back of the ten-tonne truck and pulled back the rear cover.

"Do you have any weapons in there?" shouted Todd.

"You could say that," said Andy. "Out you come, boys!" he shouted.

Fourteen fully armed uniformed soldiers jumped down from the tailgate of the truck.

"We were on our way back to camp, I figured as I was so close, I would bring a few mates round for a cuppa. Where do you want us?" he said.

Todd smiled. "This way. Quickly."

CHAPTER 39

Findlay was dragging the last of the gold to the mouth of the cave.

Preston stood watching him.

"I hope you know what you are giving up?" said Findlay.

"I'm giving nothing up," he replied. "The Manor needs hundreds of thousands spending on it. The bank book is almost empty, and I'm not going to the poorhouse for anyone. Let alone my hapless brother and my late half-witted adopted father. When this war is over and the Fuehrer walks into Buckingham palace, England will become part of Germany. I will come back. I will put that illegitimate gardener out on the street. Then I will be the lord of the Manor."

"You really have brainwashed him, haven't you?" Findlay said to Mosley.

"He's a bright boy. He knows which side will win this conflict and he will be on the winning side," he replied.

Suddenly Todd appeared at the entrance. "Good afternoon, gentlemen."

Mosley pointed the gun at him.

"Sergeant," said Findlay, "what are you doing? I sent you to get help."

"Yes sir, he said. "And I did."

Todd pointed to the cave mouth. "You'd better take a look," he said to Mosley.

Mosley slowly walked over to the entrance and, still pointing the gun at Todd, he looked over the edge.

He walked back in, now pointing the gun at Findlay. For a few moments, he stared at Findlay, then lowered the gun and handed it to Todd. "I surrender Inspector, I take it I'm under arrest?"

Findlay was bewildered and walked to the cave entrance. He looked over the edge to see fourteen British soldiers, all with their rifles pointing at the cave mouth.

Andy Mann walked in. "Top of the morning, Inspector, I could kill for a cuppa!"

Todd thanked him.

"No thanks required; I did say I would be back when you least expected me, didn't I?"

Mosley and Preston were tied securely and put into the back of the truck. Mosley smiled.

"What on earth are you smiling at?" said Preston.

"I would rather be under arrest by the police than taken to an Army base. My people will soon have us out from a rural police cell."

The gold was loaded on the truck and it continued on its way to Cockington. On arrival, it stopped outside the coroner's office.

Findlay went in and called Beth. "Come see what we have," he said.

He pulled back the cover and there was the British Army and the gold.

"But how?" she asked.

"That's a story for another day," he said with a grin. "The thieves think they are on their way to our little police station. They aren't. They are being taken to the camp. Our military police are looking forward to having a chat with Mosley. As for Preston, he's in for a rude awakening. If you grab your coat, these boys will escort you to the museum, where you can safely deliver all this history."

Todd and Findlay walked to the front of the truck. Todd reached up and shook Andy Mann's hand.

"I knew I would grow on you," said Andy.

Todd smiled, and the truck pulled away.

Andy hung out of the window. "Don't forget," he shouted, "anything you need I can get it cheap for you, from chocolates to silk stockings. I'm your man!"

Todd shook his head.

"What did he mean?" asked Findlay.

"Oh, nothing sir, nothing."

"I think we've had quite a day, Sergeant. Go home, I'll see you in the morning. We have a mountain of paperwork to do, so get a good night's sleep, and it's the Preston sentencing tomorrow. I want to be there for that."

"I'm not going to argue with you on that one, sir."

The news of the day's events soon reached the good people of Cockington, including Simonds the Chelston Manor valet. He sat alone in front of a roaring fire in the kitchen of the manor with a bottle of whiskey.

"All the years I spent looking after this family, and what do I get? Nothing! In a couple of days, that damn gardener will be here, and I'll be out on the street with nothing."

He poured himself another large glass of whiskey. "Well, I'm not having it!" he shouted, his words echoing around the empty Manor. "Do you hear me?" he shouted again. "I'm not damn well having it!"

CHAPTER 40

The following morning in the Findlay household. "You're up early this morning, dear," said Mrs F.

"Yes, I have a busy day ahead of me."

Mardie came into the kitchen. "Good morning," she said.

"Morning," said Findlay. "Seems I'm not the only one with a busy day ahead of me."

"Are you still moving up to the Manor today?" asked Mrs Findlay.

"I have to do it sometime," said Mardie. "Today's as good a day as any."

"In that case," said Findlay, "I will drive you. Are you all packed?"

"Yes," she said, "I am."

"Then we will waste no more time," said Findlay, picking up her case.

Mardie took Mrs Findlay's hand. "Thank you for looking after me," she said.

"It's been our pleasure. Don't ever feel alone," she said to Mardie. "The Manor is a big place on a cold winter's night, there's always a chair in front of our fire for you, and to be honest, I sometimes need a bit of company myself."

Mrs Findlay gave Mardie a hug. "Good luck!" she said.

Findlay pulled up at the entrance to the Manor.

"Home sweet home," he said, looking up at the building. "You are absolutely sure this is what you want?" he asked.

"Yes," said Mardy, "it is."

"I'll come in with you," he said. "Simonds is still here, I expect."

"No Inspector. Thank you, but no. I can deal with Simonds."

Findlay climbed out and opened her door. "My Lady," he said with a smile.

Mardie climbed out. She stood looking up at the Manor.

"It's all yours," said Findlay.

Mardie nodded, lifted her case and climbed the marble steps.

Findlay watched her as she pushed open the big oak door and walked inside. "Good luck," Findlay said under his breath and drove away.

Once inside, Mardie stood looking around the great hall. Paintings hung from every wall. The grandfather clock which stood in the corner chimed eight, which made her jump. She knew every corner of Chelston Manor. Every room, every secret hiding place, but she felt like a stranger as she stood in her new home.

She suddenly became aware of Simonds standing at the top of the main stairs. Mardie took a deep breath. She placed her case down and walked to the bottom of the stairs. "Can you take my case up to the blue room?" she said. "Then I would like a pot of tea in the study. We will need two cups," and she walked into the library. "Oh, and Simonds?" she shouted. "Could you make the fire in the library, please? It's chilly in here," and she closed the door behind her.

Mardie sat in the library and waited. If she was to be taken seriously, it would all depend on how Simmonds reacts to her orders. She sat and watched the old mantle clock as it ticked the minutes away.

Suddenly, the library door opened and Simonds entered, carrying a large silver tray with a teapot and two cups on it. He placed it down on the table in front of the fireplace.

"Thank you," said Mardie.

"I'll get the kindling and coals for the fire," he said.

"In a minute," said Mardie. "Please sit down, we need to talk."

Simonds slowly sat down opposite her. "I will pour, shall I?" she said.

Findlay and Todd arrived at the courts. "You go in," said Findlay. "I will park the car and be there shortly."

Todd entered the courthouse and immediately saw Alison sitting alone reading case papers. He wasn't sure if he should go over to her or not. She looked busy.

Alison suddenly looked up. "Allan," she said with the biggest of smiles, "I was hoping you would come."

"Hello," he said.

"You can sit down, I won't bite you. I was surprised when your Inspector Findlay rang me."

"Did he?" asked Todd.

"Yes, he said to meet him here at ten precisely, and you're very punctual."

"Did he indeed," said Todd.

"Why didn't he come in?" asked Alison.

"He said he was parking the car," said Todd, "but I have a feeling he won't be back here today."

"Victoria Preston is being sentenced this morning; I have to go through to the courtroom. Promise me you will be here when I come out?"

"Yes," said Todd, "of course."

"Promise me," she said.

"Ok I promise."

"Good," she said with a smile.

A little more than a half hour passed and Alison returned. "Not the outcome we wanted," she said. "Insufficient evidence. The evidence we did have was not admissible."

"So, what exactly does that mean?" asked Todd.

"She's free to go."

"What?" said Todd. "I thought it was all over bar the sentencing?"

"You never can say what the courts will decide. I think she had a few influential friends who spoke up for her. Free to go was the court's decision."

"I need to get back to Cockington," said Todd.

"I will come with you if that's okay? I have a car."

"Excellent," he said.

They made their way back to Todd's office. Findlay was just locking his car as they arrived. "Sir!" shouted Todd.

"Sergeant and Miss Thomas, what a pleasant surprise," he said with a grin.

"Not enough evidence, sir. She's been released."

Findlay said nothing. He finished locking his car. "I see," he said. "Miss Thomas, I usually find when things turn difficult, a cup of tea makes everything look clearer," he opened the door. "After you, now you, Sergeant."

They sat in Findlay's office. The silence was deafening.

Suddenly Todd said, "what about that poor girl, Mardie? We need to let her know."

"Good point," said Findlay, finishing his tea. "Right, Sergeant, and you, Miss. We need to get up to the Manor. I have a feeling the Lady Victoria will be heading up there."

They were making their way to Chelston Manor when Alison said, "it's hard to know who to trust these days."

"What do you mean?" asked Todd.

"The Preston case. I've just found out who covered the legal costs for her, a real piece of work called somebody Mosely."

"I beg your pardon?" said Findlay. "Are you saying Mosely paid her costs, would that be Oswald Mosely?"

"Yes," said Alison, "that's it, Oswald. Is that important?"

"I should say so," said Findlay. "It explains how Edward Preston and Mosely got wind of the gold, and where it was being stored. Victoria Preston must be part of their vile network of Nazi sympathisers."

"Plus," said Todd, "the Army couldn't hold them any longer and let them go."

"Put your foot down, Sergeant, get us up there fast."

Todd drove like the wind. They pulled into the drive of the Manor. Parked outside the main doors was the Late Lord Preston's Rolls Royce.

"That can only be one person," said Todd.

"Yes," replied Findlay, "she's here."

Todd pulled their car under the trees at the side of the Manor.

"I don't like the look of this," said Findlay. "You stay in the car, Miss; we will come back for you if everything is okay."

"Are you mad?" she said. "I wouldn't miss this for anything. I've not seen this much excitement since I don't know when. I'm coming with you."

"Just do us one favour," asked Todd, "stay at the back of us. We have no idea what we will find in there."

They slowly edged their way around the Manor until they reached the study.

Todd peered around the curtain. "Looks quiet enough, sir," he said.

"Try the window," said Findlay.

"I don't believe it," replied Todd. "It's open."

He slowly raised the window up and climbed in.

"Now me," said Alison.

"Can I stop you?" asked Findlay.

"No," she said. So, Findlay followed.

They slowly crept towards the study doors. Todd opened the door and looked through the crack. He turned to Findlay and said, "we seem to be making a habit of this don't we sir? It's all quiet. The kitchen is over there."

They slowly walked towards the kitchen when they heard a door slam. "It came from over there," said Alison.

"The library," said Todd.

"Wait here, both of you," said Findlay.

He opened the doors a little and there in front of him were Mardie and Simonds tied to kitchen chairs.

A man's voice rang out, "I won't ask again. Where's the safe?"

"How many times?" said Simonds. "We have no safe. Look around you, the place is falling apart. I haven't been paid in months. Look in the cupboard, it's empty. I live off vegetables from the garden and the odd handout from the village. In case you hadn't noticed, there's a war on."

"Then you leave my men no choice but to get violent. I don't want to, but I don't believe you."

Findlay couldn't believe what he was seeing. It was Oswald Mosely with two of his henchmen and Victoria Preston.

"It has to be in the study," said Victoria. "His Lordship would never allow me in there."

Mosley looked at his men. "Go and check," he said, "and look behind the pictures and curtains. The aristocracy like to be secretive."

Mosely held a gun to Mardie. "You'd better hope it's there," he said.

Findlay hid around the corner until the two men passed, then quickly made his way back to Todd and Alison. He told them what he had just witnessed.

"What are we going to do?" asked Alison.

Findlay shook his head. "I have no idea," he mumbled.

"Don't let Mosely see you, Sergeant, not after you killed two of his men."

Alison stared at Todd. "Was that you? Oh my, I had no idea it was you. Whoever would have thought it?"

"Quiet," said Findlay, "I knew we should have left you in the car."

She smiled.

"So, what now?" asked Todd.

"They want a safe. We will give them something to chase," said Findlay. "There are only three of them and three of us if we can untie Simonds."

"There's four of us," said Alison.

"No, there is not!" barked Todd. "For once, do as you're told and stay here."

"What do you have in mind, sir?"

"I will cause a diversion while you free Simmonds and Mardie."

"But sir," said Todd, "what if they catch you?"

"I'll worry about that if it happens. Wait until you hear the commotion, then it's up to you to get to the kitchen and free them."

"And you, Miss Thomas, stay here."

Findlay went as quickly and quietly as he could up the winding staircase. At the top, Findlay shouted, "it's the police, you can't escape. Lay down your weapons and sit on the floor with your hands in the air!" He then ducked around a corner.

Mosely came out of the kitchen with his gun in his hand and his two henchmen appeared from the study, looking very confused.

Mosely beckoned to his men. "Go up there and see who that is."

He went to the window and looked out across the fields. "What on earth was that about? There's nobody out there," he muttered as he walked back to the stairs.

Meanwhile, Todd had worked his way around to the kitchen. He crossed his fingers it would be clear.

It wasn't.

Lady Victoria Preston was standing looking out of the window.

Todd slowly crept in. Simonds saw Todd and gestured to him. There, hanging on a kitchen hook, was a wooden rolling pin. He knew what he had to do, even though it went against his very fibre of being a man. He couldn't risk her bringing Mosely in with his gun.

He slowly took down the rolling pin and crept towards her. He couldn't help thinking what Sally would think of him for what he was about to do.

He raised the pin up when suddenly she turned around. She was startled to see him standing behind her. Todd had a split second to react. He took the pin in his other hand, pulled back his fist, and threw a punch.

Lady Victoria instantly lost consciousness. Todd grabbed her and slowly lowered her to the floor.

"Quickly," said Mardie, "untie us."

Todd freed them from the ropes. "Nobody knows this house better than Mardie," he said to Alison. "Please," he said, "please go with her."

"Very well," she said, "but I'm warning you, if you get yourself shot, I will be furious."

Todd smiled. "Please go."

"This way," said Mardie, and they disappeared behind the kitchen fireplace.

Todd was astounded. "This old house is full of secret doors, Sergeant," said Simonds.

"Can I depend on you?" asked Todd.

"You can, Sergeant. Let's get these Nazi dogs out of Chelston Manor."

"Our first job is to get past Mosely. The Inspector is somewhere up there and one thing he isn't is a fighter."

"Follow me," said Simonds as he also went behind the fireplace.

Todd simply followed him.

"Pull that lever," said Simonds.

Todd did as instructed. The whole of the huge kitchen fireplace closed behind them.

"Try not to make any noise," said Simonds.

They began climbing steps that had been cut into the earth and rock when it was the original building.

Simmonds held up his hand. "Stop."

So Todd stood perfectly still.

Simonds whispered in Todd's ear. "We are behind a one-way mirror in the master bedroom," he said. He pointed. "Over there hiding behind the curtain. It's Findlay."

Simonds lifted a small lever and gently pushed. The mirror swung open.

"Inspector," whispered Todd, "over here."

Findlay looked on in amazement, "Sergeant?" he said, "where on earth did you come from?"

"I'll tell you later," said Todd. "Quickly, in here."

Findlay hurried across the room and joined Todd and Simonds. They slowly pulled the mirror shut just as the bedroom door opened. It was one of Mosely's henchmen.

He walked around the bedroom firstly checking behind curtains, then under the four-poster bed.

"Amateur," said Findlay.

Simonds put his hand over Findlay's mouth.

The man walked over to the mirror with an inquisitive look on his face. He looked the mirror up and down while the three men stood deathly still and watched him. Todd got himself ready. He was sure this thug was about to smash the mirror and discover their hiding place.

Suddenly, the bedroom door opened and the other man entered and said, "Hast du schon was gefunden (have you found anything yet)?"

"Nein, (No)," was the reply. "Dann mussen wir unten nachsehen (then we must go and check downstairs)."

"If we weren't sure before we are now," whispered Findlay, "they are Germans."

The two men closed the door behind them.

Simonds waited a few seconds, then released the mirror.

"Where are Mardie and Miss Thomas?" asked Findlay.

"They are safe, sir; they are in the car."

"What about Victoria Preston?

"Ah," said Todd, "I need to explain that one, sir."

Suddenly, there was a commotion downstairs. Mosely had found Victoria on the kitchen floor with blood running from the corner of her mouth. Mosely helped her to her feet and out into the Great Hall entrance.

"I know it's you Findlay!" he shouted, "and probably your pet guard dog Todd. Did you do this? Did you actually punch Lady Victoria Preston unconscious?"

Findlay looked over his glasses at Todd.

"I had no option sir, I had to."

"This way," said Simonds as he opened a linen cupboard and pulled on a coat hook, revealing yet another secret passageway. "Follow this to the end," he said, "it will bring you out at the stable block."

"What about you?" asked Todd.

"I'll be fine. They will never find me."

They did as instructed and followed the passageway to its end. Todd pushed on a door and it opened out into the morning sunlight. "Over there, Sergeant," said Findlay, pointing to the roof of the Manor.

At first, they couldn't work out who it was. Just that it was two men fighting. Suddenly, a gunshot rang out which echoed around the grounds and to their horror they saw the body of a man falling from the top of the Manor eves. They watched helplessly as the body hit the gravel drive below.

The other man stood on the edge of the roof, looking down.

"Sir," said Todd, "on the roof, that's Simonds, I'm sure of it."

They walked across the lawn towards the remains of a man. Todd bent down and rolled the body over. "It was Mosely. He's dead," said Todd. Lying next to him was his Luger pistol. Todd picked it up.

Victoria Preston and Mosely's two thugs appeared at the front of the Manor. Todd raised the Luger and pointed it. "Drop your weapons!" he shouted. "It's all over, he's dead. Do you understand me?"

One of the men pulled out a revolver and fired a shot at Todd.

Todd grabbed Findlay and threw him to the ground. He pointed his gun at them and fired.

Suddenly, Findlay's Volvo came speeding up the driveway, heading directly for the two thugs.

Victoria Preston jumped aside just as the Volvo slammed into them. Both men were sent hurtling through the air and landed on the gravel driveway.

Findlay's car skidded to a halt with smoke still coming from its tyres.

The driver's and passenger door opened and Mardie and Alison climbed out.

"That will teach them," said Alison.

Todd and Findlay got to their feet, brushing the dust from the drive from their suits.

"I don't believe you just did that," said Todd.

"Mess around with my man and you have me to deal with!" she said.

"Your man?" said Todd.

"Yes, you are my man, aren't you? If you want to be."

"Then, I suppose I am," he replied.

Findlay walked over to his car to inspect the dents. "That's going to be expensive," he said. "Sergeant, would you mind taking Lady Victoria back into custody, and use the phone in the manor to call for assistance?"

"Yes sir," he said.

"Oh, and Sergeant? Give me the gun. I wouldn't want you to hurt yourself."

"Your man?" said Findlay, looking at Alison.

She just smiled.

"Oh, by the way," she said, "I'm moving into the Manor with Mardie. She needs company and I need a bigger place. She's decided to keep Simonds on. We need a man about, so it's perfect. Plus, the added bonus of being able to keep an eye on my boyfriend."

Todd smiled and shook his head.

POSTSCRIPT

After all the excitement, Cockington village had slowly got back to normal. It was now October 1951, and the world was still recovering from years of war.

The village was just waking up. The morning mist was slowly rising above the thatched roofs as it mingled with smoke from the fires in the hearths of the cottages.

Tom Manning, the local farmer, was going about his morning and delivering milk. His route to the village centre took him past Cockington Court, which had stood empty for over twenty years. He and Benny, his faithful old cob horse, slowly clip clopped along the gravel pathway towards the village. The peacefulness of the morning was suddenly shattered by a bloodcurdling scream which came from the derelict Cockington Court.

Benny's cob froze to the spot, his ears lying flat and eyes bulging with fright. Tom spun around in his seat. "What on earth was that?" he said aloud.

He climbed down from his cart and slowly walked towards the Court. He hadn't gone far when again a scream rang out, which seemed to go straight to his very soul.

Tom turned and quickly made his way back to his cart. He jumped up and took hold of the lead rope. With one flick, he was on his way to the village.

Findlay was already at his desk sifting through the day's appointments when his office door swung open. "Tom," exclaimed Findlay, "this is a surprise. What on earth is wrong?"

"Lady Elizabeth," he gasped, "it was horrible!"

"Slow down," said Findlay. "What are you talking about?"

"The ghost of Lady Elizabeth over at the Court. I just heard her."

"Tom," said Findlay, "you do surprise me. I wouldn't have believed you would be frightened by an old wives' tale. It's just superstitious nonsense."

"I know what I heard," he said, "and it sounded real enough to me. I heard a woman scream, not once, but twice. Now, what are you going to do about it?"

Findlay smiled. "Very well Tom. I have no appointments until eleven. I'll pop over there now and have a look around."

"Good," said Tom. "I think someone should. I know what I heard, Inspector."

Findlay arranged his papers into neat piles on his desk. He put on his topcoat and hat and made his way down to his old Volvo. It was a short drive to Cockington court.

You have to be impressed, he thought to himself as he drove along the lane towards the front of the building. It had stood there for hundreds of years complete with its own private church and Norman built tower.

Findlay remembered back to that fateful day in the church when a German bomber discarded its last six-hundred-pound bomb, which landed at the back of the Court. Sally and three young mums all lost their lives that day. *Poor Sally,* he thought. *Her wedding day as well, how cruel life can be? And poor Allan Todd, the groom, his sergeant.* Findlay thought his sergeant would never recover from that day, his wedding day. It took a few years, but he finally found Alison and they had settled in the village.

Findlay reached the court. He stopped outside the arched front doorway and climbed out. He stood for a few moments, looking around the front of the house. It was quiet and peaceful, although looking neglected and run down.

Findlay walked around the side of the Court and checked the doors and windows as he went. *Well*, he thought to himself, *it all looks very quiet to me.* He was about to go back to his car when something caught his eye. He stood for a moment and stared at one of the lower back windows.

He left the path and slowly edged his way down a wet grass embankment, hoping he didn't slip; Mrs F would not be happy if he had to go home to change out of wet muddy clothes. He finally reached the bottom. Decades of dust had settled on all of the window sills, except it appeared, this one. He could see quite clearly it had been disturbed and recently.

Findlay took hold of the bottom of the window and lifted. To his amazement, it opened. He lifted his leg and swung his body inside of what obviously used to be the Court library.

The first thing that struck him was the smell of decay and rats. He stood and looked around the dozens of now empty shelves where once hundreds of books were kept. Findlay looked around at the mahogany panelling which encircled the whole room. "If only you could talk," he muttered, "what tales you could tell."

He walked over towards the library door; his every step echoed around the room. He pulled open the door and peered out into the main hallway. Findlay slowly shook his head. *What a waste,* he thought.

He stood at the bottom of a sweeping stairway which dominated the whole entrance hall. He was about to climb the stairs when he noticed that one of the many doors which ran around the entrance hall was open.

Findlay walked towards it, again every footstep sounding like a gunshot as it echoed around the house. Findlay pushed on the door, it slowly opened, creaking and cracking as it revealed what used to be the Court kitchens. It had been unloved and unused for so many years the bushes at the rear had overgrown and were blocking out what little light had managed to come through the dirt on the window glass, and yet again the unmistakable smell of damp and rats.

Findlay turned to leave when to his shock he heard a laugh, a female laughing, he thought.

He stood perfectly still and listened; all he could hear was his heart thumping. Suddenly, there it was again, a short burst of laughter which seemed to be coming from the main hallway.

He walked out of the kitchen, trying his best not to make a sound. He stood at the bottom of the stairway and looked up. There it was again, a female's laugh. "What on earth is that?" he mumbled to himself. He slowly climbed the stairs while never taking his eyes from the top of them. He reached the top and shouted, "Hello? Who's there?" but there was no answer.

Again, he shouted "Hello? This is the police. Who's there?" Still, there was no reply.

He looked around at the many doors which ran around both sides of the staircase. Suddenly, he heard it again. "Now, that's a female laughing," he said out loud. It sounded as though it was above him, but it was hard to tell as every sound echoed around the many empty rooms of Cockington Court.

Findlay pulled open the closest door to him. It was a narrow corridor with wooden stairs which stopped at the top with yet another door. He wasn't sure if you really wanted to go up there, but Findlay being Findlay, he couldn't resist the unknown.

He cautiously made his way up. At the top, he took hold of the handle and pushed it open. A cloud of dust was disturbed by the opening of the door, which he just knew would settle on his new dark suit.

He stood in the doorway and tried to look around in the dark. *It's cold up here,* he thought.

The room had only one window. He walked over to it and looked down. There was his old Volvo sitting on the gravel path. He was impressed by the panoramic view across Cockington grounds, looking over the fields to Church house farm and down onto Cockington village.

Suddenly, the quiet was shattered by the slamming of the door behind him. Findlay jumped and came out with words he would normally never use. He held his hand to his chest. His heart was beating ten to the dozen. He walked over and pulled on the handle, but it was jammed shut. He took the handle in both hands and shook it, but still it wouldn't budge.

He looked around the door frame and could see it was warped with age.

"No wonder it's jammed," he said out loud. He took hold of the handle again and was about to turn it when he suddenly felt it move.

Findlay quickly pulled back his hand and stared at the handle. Again, it moved as though somebody or something was on the other side. He took a step backwards, still staring through the gloom at the handle. It moved again. The door slowly began to open, Findlay took another step backwards. "Who's there?" he shouted, which echoed around the whole of the Court." I am a police officer. Show yourself."

There, standing silhouetted in the doorway, was a man. "Who are you?" shouted Findlay.

"Hello Inspector," the man said.

"Oh my god," said Findlay, "Andy Mann, is that really you?"

"It is, Inspector?"

"For god's sake," said Findlay, "I was expecting a headless ghost to be there. What on earth are you doing? You frightened the life out of me."

"Sorry Inspector, we had nowhere else to go. I was demobbed from the Army a year ago. I got married back in forty-five. We were alright until I lost me Army pay, then we lost our digs. We had nothing, no money, no jobs, no roof over our heads. Mrs Mann had a better offer. She took off and left us on our own. Then I remembered this place standing empty. I hoped you would just have a quick look and leave. We haven't damaged anything. I pulled some old furniture out of the back storerooms, and we got us a fire going. We sleep on a bed of old hessian sacks; they do the trick. A bit smelly but better than nothing."

"You keep saying we?" asked Findlay.

"Yes, I do, don't I? That would be me and Alice."

"Who's Alice?" said Findlay.

Andy didn't speak, he just pushed open the door. There, standing in the doorway, was a little girl. Andy took her hand. "This is Alice," he said, "my daughter, she's three."

Findlay was speechless for a few moments, then he said, "Right, at least you're not the spirit of Lady Elizabeth De' Cockington."

"Who's that?" asked Andy.

"It's of no matter," was the reply. "Get your things together," said Findlay. "You're coming with me."

"Are we under arrest?" asked Andy.

"No," replied Findlay. "I can't leave you here, apart from the fact that you're trespassing, it's no place to live. You're coming home with me."

They gathered up what little they had and Findlay put them into his Volvo. He made his way back to his house, a little worried about what Mrs F would say.

It didn't take long before they arrived. "Wait here," said Findlay. "I need to prepare Mrs F before we all walk in unannounced."

Findlay went in, but not through his usual route, the front door. He entered through the back kitchen door. Mrs F was preparing one of her famous beef stews when Findlay walked in.

"Oh my goodness," she said, "you made me jump. Why did you use the back door? You only use the back door when you've done something wrong, or it warrants a good telling off; so what have you done?"

"I haven't done anything," he said. He told her about Tom and him going to the Court. He told her about getting locked into a top bedroom and how cold and dark it was, and about the handle turning. He was about to tell her about who was on the other side of the door when she said, "don't tell me, I've had this strange feeling all day, is it Andy, Andy Mann?"

"How do you do that?" said Findlay. "How could you possibly know it would be him?"

"It's called intuition," she replied. "Woman's intuition. So where is he?"

"I'll get him," he said. "But he's not alone."

After a few minutes, Findlay returned.

"Andy!" shouted Mrs F. "How lovely to see you. It's been such a long time." And she gave him the biggest of hugs. It was then she looked over his shoulder and saw Findlay standing in the doorway holding the hand of a little girl. "My, my," she said, "who do we have here?"

"This is Alice, my daughter," said Andy.

"Alice," she said. "Alice, what a beautiful name."

"Are you hungry?" she asked.

Alice nodded.

"Then we will get you some hot food and a drink. You come over here darling and sit next to the fire."

"Andy," said Mrs F. "You sit over here. And you, 'Inspector,'" she said, looking at Findlay with a smile, "you sit here. I'll get us a pot of tea, but first I will see to Alice."

"Is that alright with you Alice?"

Alice nodded.

Mrs F attended to everyone. Alice had eaten and curled up in front of the open fire and was fast asleep. Mrs F sat down. "Right," she said, "I want to know everything. What brings you here? Why you didn't tell us you had that beautiful little girl?"

"It's a long story," said Andy.

"They are usually the best kind," said Mrs Findlay, pouring a cup of tea. "Now Andy, I'm listening?"

He told them about being discharged from the Army and how they depended on it to pay their way. "We lost our digs," he said. "If it was just me, I could lay my head anywhere, but my wife had run off. So, it was just me and Alice. I had to find us a roof, I remembered, last time I was here, Cockington Court. It was better than nothing, and it was only temporary. It would have been okay, but Alice and I were playing chase and Alice screamed a couple of times. Seems the local farmer heard us and reported it."

"I see," said Mrs F. "But why didn't you let us know you had married, and about Alice?"

"I didn't think it was fair," said Andy. "With everything Toddy had gone through, I didn't want to rub salt into the wound. I did write a couple of times, but he never replied. How is he?" asked Andy.

"He's fine, he's absolutely fine. He's still a single man, but he met Alison. She's lovely and thinks the world of him. If you would like, I'll ring him?"

"No," said Andy, "not yet."

He stood up and walked over to the fire where Alice was still sleeping. "There's more," he said.

He sat back down. Took a deep breath and said, "I'm going to die."

Mr and Mrs Findlay just sat and stared.

"What exactly do you mean?" asked Mrs F.

"It seems a packet of cigarettes has done what the German army couldn't. I have cancer."

"Oh, my god Andy! Have you had tests? Have you been to a hospital? They can do all kinds of things these days."

"I've done everything I can do," he said quietly. "There's nothing that can be done for me, it's just a matter of time."

Mrs F reached over and took his hand. "Andy," she said, "what can we do to help? You only have to ask."

Andy smiled. "I'm glad you said that," he replied. "I want you to take Alice into your home and take care of her."

"That's a hell of an ask," said Findlay.

"I know," replied Andy. "Alice is all I have; she has no idea what is to come. My time is very limited. I have to be sure Alice will be alright. I will not have her going into the Torquay orphanage. I needed somebody I could trust. Somebody I know will look after my little girl, and I wouldn't trust anybody like I would trust you and Mrs F."

Mrs F turned and looked at Findlay. She gave a little smile and nodded.

Findlay stood up and walked over to the kitchen window. He stood for a few moments, hands clasped behind him, cleared his throat and said, "very well, yes will take Alice in."

Mrs F smiled and put her arms around Andy. "It will be fine," she said. "Your little girl will be safe with us."

"Thank you," said Andy, "thank you."

"Did they say how long you have?" asked Mrs F.

"It's not long," said Andy. "Maybe a few weeks."

"Weeks?" replied Findlay.

"Yes, it was months, but that was a while ago. I haven't told Alice," he said, "she wouldn't understand. She knows I go off for work. I will be going off to work in a few days, I've told her. I won't be coming back. I don't want her to have to go through what's to come. An old Army mate of mine will put me up and look after things when the time comes. I will give him your name and details; he will let you know when it's all over."

"You've given it a lot of thought."

"I have, yes," he replied. "So now I would like to go and see Toddy."

"I'll ring him for you," said Mrs F.

"Tell him I'll meet him at that cave where we stopped that Mosely fella in about an hour. Can I leave Alice with you?"

"Of course," said Mrs F. "This is her home now, and yours, Andy."

He smiled. "Thank you," he said, and left from the kitchen door.

Mrs Findlay rang Sergeant Todd. "Allan," she said, "I have a surprise for you. Your friend Andy is here. He wants to meet you at a cave. He said you would know which one, very strange. Oh, and he said something about a man called Mosely."

"I know where he means, Mrs F, thank you."

At first, Todd wasn't going to go. He thought back to that day years ago when Andy Mann and his friends saved their lives. He decided he owed him. "Least I can do is meet him," he muttered.

He made his way up to the cave; Andy was sitting at the entrance, looking out to sea. He stood up and outstretched his hand. "Toddy," he said, "it's good to see you. It's been a long time."

"Yes," replied Todd, "it has. What brings you to Devon?"

Andy told him of his illness.

"Damn," said Todd. "That's real bad luck. Is there nothing that can be done?"

"No," he replied, "nothing. I've never really trusted anybody," said Andy, "not until I met you at Aldershot station, and then I met Inspector and Mrs Findlay. I'm going to tell you something, Toddy, because I know I can trust you. That day when we came up here and stopped that Nazi Pig, there was gold and jewels everywhere. I couldn't resist it. I picked up a handful of coins, gold coins. I buried them in that far corner, all except one, which I put in my pocket. I've been carrying it around for years. I know a bloke in London. He said he will buy them all from me."

"Really?" said Todd. "Are they still there?"

"I don't know, I haven't looked."

"Then I suggest you do," said Todd.

Andy walked across the fine yellow sand to the corner of the cave. He bent down and began scooping out the sand. Suddenly, he stopped. He pulled out his hand, holding nine solid gold coins. He walked towards Todd at the cave mouth and held out his hand.

Todd took one. "Well I never," he said. "They must be worth a fortune. Why are you showing me this?"

"I'm going to die, Toddy old boy. I don't want to meet my maker as a thief. I wanted to sell these coins to secure Alice's future."

"Who's this Alice?" asked Todd.

"My daughter, she's three. Her mum ran off nearly two years ago. I'm all she's got, and I've got nothing to leave her, just the memory of her dad, the thief. Inspector and Mrs Findlay have agreed to take her in."

Todd said nothing. He turned and looked out to sea. Andy stood and waited to see what Todd was going to do.

Todd turned around. "You know I can't let you take these, don't you? But I understand what you're telling me. I will pass these coins onto Beth the coroner. I'll tell her I found them in the cave. The finder's fee will be considerable. I will see that the fee is put into a bank for your daughter. At least you can meet Saint Peter with a clear conscience."

Andy smiled. "Thank you. I just knew I could trust you and that you could help me." And handed him the coins.

Todd put them in his pocket. "Come with me," he said," there's someone special I want you to meet. You can introduce us to your daughter."

The two men made their way to Cockington village. They had just reached the clock tower when a car horn sounded. It was Findlay in his trusted old Volvo, and sitting next to him was Alison. "Jump in," he said. "Mrs F is waiting for us."

They arrived at Findlay's cottage and gathered in the kitchen.

Todd and Alison were sitting at the kitchen table when Mrs F came in, holding Alice's hand.

"This is Alice."

Alice smiled.

"Oh," said Alison, "you're beautiful. Can I pick you up?"

Alice put out her arms, and she picked her up.

"Why don't you show her the flowers in the garden, I would like a quick word with Allan."

Findlay, Alison, and Andy took her into the garden.

Mrs F sat down in front of Todd. "That little girl is about to become an orphan. We will do whatever we can for her, but at our age her life won't be very exciting. She needs a proper home, a home filled with love, and people she can depend on for the rest of her life. It's been many years since you lost Sally. You've been blessed with another chance in the way of Alison. Maybe it's time you learned to live again while you still have the chance? Think about what I've said, Allan."

He took a deep breath. "I will," he said.

"Good," said Mrs F, "I'll put the kettle on, shall I?"

The door opened, and they all sat at the kitchen table with Alice holding on tightly to Alison.

Alison sat quietly and stroked Alice's hair.

Todd sat deep in thought, watching her.

Suddenly Todd stood up. "Alison," he said sternly, "I love you. Will you marry me?"

Everybody was astounded, they just sat and stared at her.

"Not quite how I imagined it," she said, "but, yes, I will!"

The whole table cheered and congratulated them.

Findlay looked over at Mrs F and winked. She simply smiled.

"One other thing," said Todd. "If you are agreeable, Andy, and the Inspector and Mrs Findlay have no objections? We will see a solicitor tomorrow and start the adoption procedure for Alice. Is that alright with you?"

Alison looked at him and smiled. She simply said, "I love you Allan Todd."

THE END

KEN MACKENZIE

K en Mackenzie is a bestselling author of many children's books with many talents to his name. Whether it's his long-standing work with the Children's Hospice South West, his beautiful piano playing that transports listeners all around his hometown of Torquay or his children's stories; he takes people on a journey to a brighter, kinder world.

Mardie and the Cockington Gold is the second book in the Inspector Findlay mystery series novel, inspired by his daily dog walks around the beautiful Cockington Village and grounds of Cockington Court.

TURN YOUR BOOK DREAMS INTO REALITY

Do you have a story that you tell your kids and grandkids all the time? Are your friends and family always telling you, "you should be an author"?

Old Mate Media is a specialist publishing company that can help you take your creative thoughts from scribblings to a published book. We walk with authors along the publishing road, stepping in to offer our expertise only where it's needed, so you can create a beautiful and affordable published book.

Visit <u>oldmatemedia.com</u> to find out how we can help you realise your dream.

Milton Keynes UK
Ingram Content Group UK Ltd.
UKHW022002050524
442194UK00005B/259